WEAVING
MAGIC

by

Mindy Hardwick

Cover Art: Serious Take Productions
Layout and Book Design by Kelly Shorten, KMD Web Designs

E-book Published by MuseItUp Publishing, April 2012

Eagle Bay Press
Lake Stevens, Washington

ISBN 13: 978-0-692425-63-3
ISBN 10: 0-692425-63-2

EAGLE BAY PRESS

DEDICATION

For the sober addict

CHAPTER ONE

Shantel

I read the letter and stuck it in my purse. My heart pounded but there was nothing I could do about any of it right now. The best thing was to pretend nothing was wrong, just like I always did when trouble found me. I pasted a smile on my face and pulled open the screened back door of the bakery. The smell of freshly baked bread and coffee brewing always made me grateful Mia owned a bakery and not something like a fish market. I spent a lot of time at the bakery. Mia relied on me to help out when she had to be at home with baby Owen. I didn't mind so much. After I'd pop the muffins or scones into the oven, I could usually steal a few minutes to work on homework.

I grabbed an apron from the red hook by the large stove and slipped my purse under the counter. Tying the apron around my waist, I made my way to the front. Funny, there were no customers. Usually, on a Saturday morning, the bakery was packed. But before I could say anything, Mia appeared in front of me with a tray of chocolate truffles. Her dark curly hair framed her round face, and her eyes were shadowed with dark circles.

"Try one?" she asked.

"Mmm…" I took one of the chocolate balls, as the bright red painted tulip on the tray caught my eye. Mia believed tulips should be everywhere. Tulips sat in small, red and blue vases on the round bakery tables. Tulip pictures covered the walls of the bathroom—both men and women. There were even sugar cookies in the shape of tulips. Mia thought tulips were the best way to remind people the small valley town had something special to share.

Local folks knew if it weren't for the tulip festival, tourists would never stop in Riverview. They would just keep driving past on their way up to the Canadian Border. But every spring, around Easter, the annual Tulip Festival drew millions of people to the fields to snap pictures of the colorful red and yellow blooms. People crowded the shops and restaurants, and sometimes, some of them returned later in the year to enjoy a peaceful weekend strolling around the brick buildings and poking into the boutique and antique shops.

The chocolate oozed around inside my mouth and I bit back a moan. Mia never made chocolate truffles unless there was something special, like a wedding or an engagement party. She always said chocolate was too much work for a small bakery. "What's the occasion?"

"It's for… "Mia bit down on her lip and swallowed hard. Her face paled and the dark circles seemed to stand out even more.

I touched Mia's shoulder gently. I loved Mia and I never liked to see her hurting. She was only eight years older than me and more like a sister than an aunt. But Mia and I handled life very differently. Now, as her shoulders shook. I wanted to tell her to just pretend life worked out. Pretend everything was fine. Just like when we were kids, and Mia and I pretended to set up our own bakery. And look what happened. Mia owned the best bakery in town.

Wasn't it enough for chocolate candy to be delicious? Did we really have to talk about the reason for the chocolates? I picked up a paperback romance lying on the counter. I moved my tongue over my lips, in what I thought might pass for a slow, sensual movement the authors wrote in the romance stories I loved. I even let out a small sigh as if the chocolate was as good as a kiss. I didn't ever tell anyone that, although I am fifteen, the only kissing I ever did was at Adam's seventh grade party. And that kiss was only because Adam made a mistake in the dark and thought I was Courtney. When he found out it was me, he quickly pulled away and muttered something like, "Wrong girl," before he scrambled towards the kitchen. Mortified, I pretended Adam really did like me, and he'd just needed to run to the kitchen for a glass of water.

"I miss her," Mia said. "I know the chocolates won't bring her back. But…" She blinked back a small tear in the left corner of her eye. "I just miss her."

Stop. I wanted to reach out and shake Mia. Just stop. We don't have to talk about this. We can play the pretend game. My pulse pounded. We needed to play the pretend game. "What's this about?" I asked brightly as I flipped the pages of the paperback. "A pirate who captures a maiden? Two people who hate each other and are stranded at an inn by a snow storm? You know the last one we read was really good." Play along with the pretend game, I pleaded silently. Please. Pretend. It will all be better if we can just pretend.

Mia pulled out a tissue from her apron pocket, and blew her nose. The tissue looked pretty scruffy and I thought she could use a new one. Quickly, I turned and grabbed my purse from under the counter. I loved my bag. I'd found the scrap material in an old costume box left outside the children's theater. 'Free' was printed in bold black letters across the top. It'd been easy to sew it together, and the purse was roomy enough to fit everything—especially my romance paperbacks.

I grabbed a bag of tissues and my tablet. I couldn't wait to show Mia how I would be reading the romances. "Look what I bought," I said as I pressed the on button. "Do you know how many romance books I can hold at one time?" I'd already loaded the reader with five romance e-books.

"I like my books," Mia said, and sniffed.

"But, this keeps what I read secret." I winked. Everyone always assumed that, as the State Science Champion of the Year, I would be reading something scientific and factual. But my favorite stories where about kind Sebastian sweeping independent and feisty Cassandra off her feet. Mia introduced me to the world of romance. It didn't take much to hook me, and I convinced Mia to form a book club that only read romance. Each month, we met at the bakery and dove into the steamy love stories. Romance book club was my favorite part of the month. I could have lived and breathed romance books. "So what are we reading this month?"

Mia wiped her eyes, and tucked the tissue back into her pocket. "I'm not sure about the title, but I think the main character is a scientist." Mia slid the chocolates off the tray onto a thin platter.

"Perfect." I'd been dreaming how, one day, my own Sebastian would walk into my life, and I'd have my happily ever after. Oh, we'd probably fight at first isn't that what happened in all romance stories? But then, we'd see how happy we made each other, and live happily ever after.

Mia reached under the counter and pulled out a small stack of gold embossed paper cups. She sat down on a red stool, behind the counter, and began to wrap each piece of chocolate in the paper. With her left hand, Mia pushed the paper cups toward me.

"Where is everyone this morning?" The tables didn't have a single crumb or used cup on them. The tins of coffee were all still full.

"Street fair," Mia said.

"Right!" I was supposed to help at the Children's Theater Street Tent. I took a quick look at the watch on my wrist. The watch bracelet was a gift from Dad and I rarely took it off. On my thirteenth birthday, we had gone into Seattle and spent the day walking through Fremont and Wallingford looking for just the right gift. When we'd gotten home, instead of lying in bed, Mom made dinner and set the table with her special blue and gold china. That day was one of the good days.

"Shantel," Mia said softly. "If you want to talk…"

"I'm fine." I waved my hand airily at her. "You know," I said, "today could be the day when I find my happily-ever-after."

Mia only gave me one of her looks, and I grimaced at her. Finding a happily ever after was much easier than thinking about those chocolate truffles or letters.

By the time the town square clock chimed one o'clock, I was a sweaty mess and we'd run out of the stepping stones at the Children's Theater street fair tent. Both the theater's manager, Gloria, and I had been busy since the booth opened. Children and parents packed the tables and I didn't see how either one of us could leave to fetch more stones from the hardware store across town.

On the other side of the booth, Gloria helped a young girl insert a broken dish piece into mortar on a stone. The girl's anxious mother stood nearby. My throat closed and I quickly looked away.

Don't think about it, I admonished myself, and smiled at Gloria. Unlike Mia, Gloria would not pester me about today. Gloria and Mia had been best friends for as long as I could remember. They attended high school together, and both decided to stay in Riverview. Gloria ran the Children's Theater and always needed to raise money for the shows. Each year, Gloria thought of a different art project for kids and their parents. The projects were collected during the day and, at night, sold at a hundred dollar a plate auction. Last year, we used blank canvases people could paint. The year before Gloria found a local glass artist who was willing to teach people how to blow glass balls. Although that hadn't really worked too well, as most people wanted to keep their glass balls and not auction them off.

I lifted a stepping stone onto the table, took a step backward, and promptly crashed into a warm chest.

"Umfh," I managed. Embarrassed, I stepped away and looked up into bright blue eyes, and a face that was instantly familiar.

"Christopher," I breathed.

I could never forget Christopher. I'd met him two years ago as an eighth grader. By a strange twist of good luck, Christopher had been my partner in French. Every time he looked at me, or our hands accidentally touched, I knew he liked me. I couldn't wait until the year-end dance. I'd been dreaming about it since December. Christopher would take my hand, and lead me out to the dance floor. He'd wrap his arms around me and tell me I was the only girl for him. Of course, we'd be together forever.

But things hadn't exactly happened that way. Instead, the dance had barely started before Christopher disappeared like a magic trick. I spent most of the night trying to pretend I was having a good time when, in reality, all I could do was wonder what happened to him. It was one time when, I have to admit, the game of pretend did not work very well. When the dance ended, we all rushed outside, only to find Christopher being escorted into a police car. He could barely stand and the rumors immediately started he'd been caught using drugs. I refused to believe it. Not the Christopher I knew. He'd never use drugs.

But by the fall, Christopher was gone. Everyone said his mom had him transferred to the private high school. I had been devastated. All my dreams of being with Christopher in high school were shattered.

Now, here he was, and I could barely breathe.

"Hi," Christopher said, and smiled at me. "Good to see you." He touched my arm briefly and shivers ran up and down my insides. It was fate that we met again.

Fate.

Christopher absently picked up a spatula covered with hardened mosaic goop. "Ladies and Gentleman." He waved the pretend wand in the air.

Immediately, a small crowd gathered outside the tent. I smiled. It was just like eighth grade. Christopher was charming everyone. I stood a little taller next to him.

Christopher inserted his ungloved hand into a plastic bucket and scooped up a large handful of mortar. He rubbed the mortar over his hand. The thick gooey substance spread between his fingertips.

"Wait...I wouldn't..."

"Yes?" Christopher raised his eyebrow at me.

I giggled. Christopher looked just like our French teacher, Mrs. Pierce, who gave us a similar look when we flubbed another French word and turned it to garble. "Mortar hardens fast," I managed to say, as I grabbed a rag from the back table.

Christopher waved his hand in the air as if a hand covered with hardening mortar was all part of the show. A gaggle of giggling ten-year-old girls inched closer to him. How many other girls had Christopher entertained since I'd last seen him? Was there someone who he called a girlfriend?

"I'm a statue!" Christopher froze. He raised his hands to the sky. Out of the corner of his mouth, he whispered, "Hand me that rag." He winked at me. "I think I may have gotten myself in a mess."

Quickly, I grabbed the turpentine and cloth Gloria kept on the back table. Christopher reached out for a stepping stone and sent them crashing to the ground.

I froze.

Everyone in the tent turned to stare at us. I knew my face was turning shades of purple. I hated being the center of attention. It was okay for things like Science Fair award ceremonies where I only had to shake someone's hand and take the ribbon. But to be center stage because of something bad was unthinkable.

"I'll fix it," Christopher muttered as he leaned over and lifted the broken pieces from the ground. They were equal in size. It was as if someone had taken a knife and simply sliced down the middle. I was mesmerized by his hands and the gentle way he held the stones. What would it feel like to be in his hands, being held so gently? I shivered.

Christopher dropped a glob of mortar over one of the half-moon stones. He plunked broken slices of china into the soft white mortar. When he was finished, he held up the stone. "Two for the price of one," he said and smiled at me with a gentle, lazy, sexy look. My heart crashed to the ground like the broken pieces. Christopher had me hooked. I would have done anything he asked at that moment.

"Thanks," I mumbled.

"See you later, Sarah," Christopher said as he strolled out of the tent.

Sarah?

No, I shook my head.

He must have said Shantel.

I simply misheard.

CHAPTER TWO

Christopher

I hopped into my truck and drove out of the church parking lot. I was hungry after the morning AA meeting, and wanted to grab something to eat. The street fair seemed like the place with the most choices. The tantalizing smells wafted into the church basement windows for the last hour, while I tried to keep my mind on things like the Serenity Prayer. My stomach had growled so loudly a couple of the guys looked over at me and told me to keep it down.

I'd already eaten two burritos, and was on my way to the Greek Gyro stand, when I saw the Children's Theater tent. One of the things I needed desperately was a job. When I used to be on the baseball team, Mom and Dad never mentioned a job. Baseball was my job and Mom always took care of my car insurance and car payments. But as soon as I got back from rehab, the first thing Mom said to me was, "You need to get a job. Your dad and I are not paying for any more of your bills. The rehab bill was big enough."

I knew it was expensive to send me to rehab and Mom's job as a real estate agent wasn't bringing in much money anymore. Mom and Dad were always huddled in some corner, poring over the bank statements and bills. When I was playing ball, everyone knew I would get a fullride scholarship to any college. But all that changed. Now I had to start figuring out what I wanted to do with the rest of my life. Or so my guidance counselor at school liked to tell me.

I thought checking out the theater was a good start. I liked the theater when I was little, and maybe there were things I could do, like building sets or janitorial projects.

I didn't count on running into Sarah. As soon as I saw her, I knew she remembered me. But I didn't have a clue who she was. It wasn't unusual for me not to remember people. I'd done a lot of blacking out when I was using. But the way Sarah acted—I thought it was Sarah—I was pretty sure we'd known each other well, and I had to play it cool. I thought I did pretty well. She seemed to really like my whole impromptu show and that made me feel good. And when I accidentally knocked off the stepping stones, I found a way to fix everything. I tapped my fingers on the steering wheel, hummed, and turned onto my street.

I saw the cop car when I was three houses away. Its lights weren't flashing, but the car was still sitting smack in the middle of our driveway. Immediately, the sweat started building on my palms. Breathe. Just breathe. I was no stranger to cop cars. My first experience occurred at the eighth grade dance. I'd taken the pill Michael gave me, and the next thing I knew, I was in the back of some cop car with the world spinning. But I hadn't been down that path lately. Not for the last eighty-five days, and I wasn't planning to go that way again.

I parked my truck in front of the house. Someone sat inside the back of the cop car. I wanted to believe it was Michael. Michael lived three houses down from me, and although I've been in and out of treatment, he hasn't yet.

But, if it was Michael, they'd be at his house, not ours.

I stepped out of the truck, and walked toward the house, the cops were talking with Mom at the door. Alex huddled up beside Mom, and I realized who must be in the cop car.

Dad.

This was a dream. It had to be a bad dream. I wanted to talk to him, but, as I got closer, the officer shook his head at me. I raised my eyes and looked at Dad through the glass window.

He mouthed the word, "Magic."

I nodded like I understood what he meant, and then walked away with my gaze straight ahead. It was as if I were walking with a gun at my back, and someone kept urging me to keep moving. I stopped when I reached the front door.

"Christopher." Mom reached out and grabbed me. I jerked away. There were white spots on my arm from her fingers.

I pushed past both Mom and the cop.

Magic.

I had to get Dad's magic box.

There must be something inside the magic box.

Something important.

I dropped my house keys into the small basket by the front door. "Remember to keep your keys in the basket," Mom constantly reminded me. "We might need to make a mad dash out of the house." She always tries to make light of her efforts to control me. And I pretend not to mind. But I felt the stab inside all the same, and wonder if she would ever trust me again.

I did borrow her car. Once. Okay, maybe twice. And yes, I admit, I didn't have my license yet. But I've made amends for those times. I wished she'd just let it go.

I headed upstairs. Mom mumbled something to the cop before she shut the door with a bang. She was crying and Alex was asking, "But when can he come home? When?"

In a matter of minutes I heard the clink of glass as Mom got out the wine bottle. It's not that I minded—too much. Mom has always enjoyed wine, and right now, I couldn't say that I blamed her. I would have liked a good glass of wine myself. I'd have slugged it down in one gulp. Numb the feelings inside.

At Family Week, the counselors said the addict's decision to stay sober rests with the addict.

No one else.

One speaker talked about his family and how they were all going to their Meetings. He told us how great it was to have the family share recovery. My dream of Mom, Dad, and Alex at Meetings barely had time to get off the ground before Mom made it very clear that "this staying sober business" was my problem. She and Alex didn't need Meetings. Later, Dad pulled me aside and said he would go to a Meeting, just to check it out. But that never happened. Something always seemed to get in the way. Usually it was long hours at his accounting job, or sometimes it was Alex's soccer game. I tried to pretend I didn't mind.

I walked into my room and opened the closet door. It's a big closet. When I was a kid, I liked to make forts in the closet out of sleeping bags, chairs and blankets. When I was using, it was a great place to store my stuff. Now, it was just a closet.

I maneuvered around a large moving box. It wasn't a box I wanted to open. When I got home from rehab, I shoved my baseball comforter and desk lamp into the box. The room screamed I'd become a loser and a disappointment. It was a constant reminder of how I wasn't a star on the ball field. Instead, I'd had the bad luck to be in the first class for Cascadia High School's new athletic policy which said: An athlete could be tested for drugs. If the urinalysis came up dirty, the athlete would be removed from the team with recommendations for further treatment. I was nailed as the first athlete with a dirty UA.

At the back of my closet, I grabbed a small flimsy black box from a tiny shelf which looked like it should hold shoes. I carefully lifted the box from the shelf. Things like cups and balls, a plastic chicken, and a plastic rope were inside the box. When I was young, Dad taught me the easy tricks like sleight of hand, cups and balls, and how to make plastic chickens disappear. He always talked about teaching me how to do the big tricks. But somehow, we never found the time. Now I wondered if that time was gone forever.

I carefully balanced the box in my right hand and slowly backed out of the closet. Once I was fully out of the closet, I spilled the box's items onto the floor, and looked for something— anything. A piece of paper. Drugs. Something to let me know why Dad was in that cop car. It didn't matter what it was. Whatever it was, I would take it, and hide it. Destroy the evidence.

But as I combed through the items on the carpet, right away I could see there was nothing which wasn't supposed to be there.

I picked up a soft, pink ball and rubbed it in my hands. The last time I performed any of the tricks was for kids at the local hospital. It was community service hours for my ninth-grade civics class. I enjoyed watching the kids' faces light up. Even after the community service hour requirements ended, I continued showing up at the hospital once a week and performing.

But the temptation to scoop up a few medicines on the way out the door became too easy. One of the nurses saw me trying to swipe a couple pills. She suggested strongly that I find somewhere else to volunteer.

The magic tricks in the box weren't difficult to do. It was just a matter of diverting the audience's attention somewhere else. A little like an addict diverting the attention somewhere else so we can use. Is that what Dad was trying to tell me? Divert the attention somewhere else? But why was he trying to divert the attention somewhere else? I stared at the new carpet on the floor. The carpet was just installed last week. Mom and Dad got in a big fight. Mom demanded to know where Dad got the money. Dad told her not to worry. Now I had an awful feeling in the pit of my stomach.

A loud thump outside my bedroom jolted me out of my thoughts. Standing, I walked to the window. "Alex," I hollered. "Stop!"

Alex gave me an evil eye and kicked the ball one more time. This time it flew up toward my window, and landed just inches below with a loud thump. Alex was eight years younger than me, and while I looked more like Dad, Alex was the spitting image of Mom. He has her same yellow blonde hair, bright blue eyes, and round face. Alex has never been interested in baseball. And I didn't blame him. It must be hard to want to get involved in a sport when your older brother ended up in treatment because he was a druggie. I wasn't exactly older-brother role model of the year.

I slammed the window shut. The next thing I knew, Alex appeared at my bedroom doorway. His green t-shirt was stained with dirt. His jean shorts hugged his small legs too tightly. I wondered if Mom noticed he was outgrowing his clothes again.

"What's that?" He asked and pointed toward the magic box. "You got drugs in that box?"

I cringed. It was true; at one time I might have hidden drugs in the box. But not now.

"No," I said loudly. "I don't have drugs in that box."

"Dad got arrested," Alex stated.

"I know."

"Drugs?"

"I don't know." I stared at the magic items scattered on the floor. There were no answers to Dad's arrest.

CHAPTER THREE

Shantel

Sebastian's warm fingers traced lightly along the side of my face and I shivered. Tenderly, he cupped my chin. His deep-set, chocolate-brown eyes gazed into mine as he whispered, "Cassandra." I couldn't lift my eyes from him and felt myself surrender against his firm and strong body. "Sebastian," I moaned.

I snuggled deeper into my thick pillows and clicked the page button on my tablet. My clock glowed 7:33 a.m. Cleo, my calico cat, curled by my feet. I'd been up since five working on my SAT online prep class. Dad called it my summer of productivity. I called it my summer of insanity. I was taking two advanced summer classes at Cascadia, the online SAT Prep class, volunteering at the children's theater, helping Mia in the bakery, and weaving scarves to sell on consignment. Dad thought it was all a part of being a high school student who excelled. "Colleges look at these things," he said. "Volunteering. Working. SAT scores and Advanced classes. Talents. These activities will place you ahead of the pack."

Sometimes I just wanted to be a part of the pack.

The problem was, Dad never factored in my other commitment—the farm. It was my job to make the strawberry and blueberry jam we sold at the summer markets all over the County. It was also my job to balance the farm finances, a chore that was getting harder and harder to do.

I glanced at my purse where I dropped it the night before. The letter was still tucked inside. It wasn't the first one we received, and I knew we couldn't ignore it.

I shifted my legs under the patchwork quilt. Cleo stirred but didn't open her eyes. Why couldn't things be as easy as a romance novel?

At my bedroom doorway, Dad cleared his throat. "That's my girl. Getting a head start on her class." He brushed a thin strand of mostly grey hair away from his narrow forehead. I made a mental note to be sure and schedule a hair appointment. I scheduled a lot of things like hair appointments and making sure we went to the dentist two times a year. It was only one more of the things I'd been doing ever since, well, ever since she's been gone.

Guiltily, I slipped the reader under the quilt. "I didn't hear you."

"I brought you something." Dad dropped three heavy text books onto my desk. "I thought you might like some advanced reading."

"Sure." I eyed the stack of books. I hadn't started to read the books he'd brought me last week. Ever since I was in elementary school, Dad filled my bookshelves with everything from how things worked, to the types of plants indigenous to the Northwest. He said it was easy to sift through the used books at the college bookstore and pick up a few titles for me.

Most of the time, I enjoyed the books. After I read them, we spent hours talking about the unfamiliar concepts. But, now my tablet was loaded up with romance, I couldn't read the science books and all the romance novels. I flushed. I didn't want to talk about Sebastian and Cassandra with Dad.

Dad wandered to the large floor loom which I'd placed next to the window that overlooked the farm. "Is this your latest?" Dad touched the black and white threads warped on the loom.

"Yes." I popped out of bed and scurried over to the loom. Cleo jumped off the bed and trotted out of the room. "It's called a double weave. The scarf has been selling pretty well." I tried to learn a new weave every month. Some of the experiments did better than others. My worst disaster had been a honeycomb waffle weave. I didn't tighten the weave enough and the scarf unraveled. The customer returned with an angry declaration, informing me she knew buying scarves made by a teenager was a mistake. I'd been mortified, and immediately offered her three free scarves of my most basic twill weave. It seemed to calm her, and a few weeks later, she'd been back to buy another scarf.

Usually, I set aside my scarf money in a special account for college. But this time, I'd slipped the money into an envelope and kept it under my mattress until I had enough for the tablet. I already knew buying romance stories online would be easier than trying to get copies at the library. The library had a limited collection, and, most of the time, they were reserved for months. I relied on the books Mia purchased and then passed on to me. But now, with the digital, I could get my own copies.

"I'm so proud of you." Dad pointed towards the small box of scarves, each wrapped in tissue paper, sitting on the floor net to the loom. "I'm seeing Kathi tonight for dinner. I'll bring her the scarves."

The room went dark and something terrible pounded in my chest. Something terrible I did not want to think about.

Go to the happy place, I said to myself. Happy place. Not the dark and scary one. Happy place. Sebastian and Cassandra. I moved a long strand of curly hair, which had slipped out of my silver barrette clip, away from my cheeks. I ran my tongue over my bare lips. My lips were absent of any frosted color that might be kissed away in a passionate and steamy embrace. It wasn't like me to wear heavy make-up. I didn't like the way thick foundation or blush felt against my skin. It always felt as if something was being clogged by all that goop. And, I couldn't help remembering the way Christopher looked at me as he fixed the broken mosaic stone. What would it feel like to have Christopher Parks kissing my bare lips and running his hands through my thick dark hair?

Of course, that would be after I clarified the fact my name was Shantel, and not Sarah. He was probably one of those people who remembered faces but not names. I'd tell him my name and we'd both have a good laugh.

"Shantel," Dad said at the same time my cell phone buzzed.

Quickly, I scurried over to my purse and hunted for my phone. Once I grabbed it, I mouthed, "Drew" to Dad.

"Fifteen minutes. I'll give you a ride over to Cascadia."

I nodded and answered the phone. "Are you at class yet?" Drew asked.

"No." I sank down into the desk chair and stared at the large stack of books in front of me. Drew was my long-time and faithful science partner. He thrived on competition and pressure. He'd been competing with me—in a friendly way, he always made sure to say— since we were in fifth grade. Drew had been telling me for weeks how lucky I was to be allowed in the summer physics class at Cascadia. He wished he'd gotten a chance to be in the class. We both knew Dad's connections at the University earned me the one open spot. Dad also pulled a few strings so I could take an advanced literature class. I'd already gotten the syllabus, and it was mostly about reading various fairy tale interpretations.

Drew didn't want to know anything about the literature class. He wanted my physics syllabus and for me to tell him each experiment we did.

"I thought you'd be there already," Drew said.

"Class doesn't start for an hour. I'm a little nervous."

"It'll be fine." Drew brushed over my fears the way he always did whenever I admitted them. Unlike Mia, who seemed to want to talk about things I didn't want to remember, Drew never asked me any questions. Instead, we always talked about science and things that could be debated and proved, based on factual information. Drew didn't understand the pressure of being Dad's daughter. He didn't understand failure was not an option. Neither was making my own choices. I lived by Dad's expectations. Period.

"Who will be my lab partner?" I asked Drew.

"You've won every Science competition since you were in fifth grade. There won't be a problem."

I couldn't help it. I glowed with Drew's praise. I'd been winning science fairs since I was ten, and not all of it had to do with Dad's expectations. Some of that had to do with me. My ability to compete and win.

"I want a full report," Drew continued. "Tell me everything that happens."

"Of course," I said. "You know I tell you everything."

CHAPTER FOUR

Christopher

"Yo." Michael glided out from behind Cascadia's main office like a vampire about to taste his prey. It was the first day of summer school, and I was in a hurry. I didn't really have time to talk. After the AA meeting, I helped pick up the folding chairs and washed out the coffee pot. The Old Timers in AA call it "being of service." I called it something to distract myself so I didn't have to go home and see Mom. All she did was sit at the kitchen table, in her blue bathrobe, sucking down another cup of coffee while she scribbled furiously in a journal, and ignored the ringing phone. It was only two days since Dad's arrest, but the papers got hold of the story. The phone rang all the time and I had to dodge reporters knocking at the door at all hours. Mom walked around tight-lipped and wouldn't say anything. She handed us frozen dinners and instructed us to heat them up, and then spent long hours on the computer looking up things like sentences, and jail times. I admit, I hopped onto the computer, and looked up a few things myself. But without really know why Dad got arrested, and Mom not talking about it, it was hard to find out what might be going on.

And now I was late for the first day of summer school, which is not a good way to start, considering I was trying to show everyone I had begun a new life. I wanted everyone to see I was responsible and that meant showing up for class on-time. I also didn't want to listen to a bunch of questions about Dad. I could imagine what people would say to me. First you, now your Dad. What's with the Parks family? A bunch of screwups. No, I didn't want to listen to the questions.

But, I couldn't just walk away from Michael either. Michael's brown, greasy hair hung low over his forehead. His eyes were hidden behind thick, dark sunglasses. I didn't have to lift them to know what was underneath. Diluted pupils and heavy, red-rimmed eyes. He looked so much like a vampire I half-expected him to swing a black cloak over his shoulders, and bare his fanged teeth.

"Yo." I said, in what has been our greeting since Michael and I became friends in kindergarten. Both of us were unable to sit still in story time. Miss Song, our patient and kind teacher, became exhausted trying to manage both of us. She finally tossed us together in time-out. It was the beginning of what turned out to be a long career in time-outs.

"Going somewhere?"

"Class." The AA members called a former drug dealer "shaky ground." They advised me to "change people and places" if I wanted to stay sober. I didn't mean to make excuses, but I could see how, as an adult, it might be possible. But as a teen, well, I wasn't so sure. I had a year left before I graduated. Changing schools wasn't an option. I needed to make things work. And this morning, that meant talking to Michael.

"Got a little something." Michael slipped his right hand into his jeans pocket, and without missing a beat, said slyly, "If you're interested."

I knew this dance, had seen him do it a hundred times. "Got a little something," meant I'll give you a trial and you'll be back for more. You'll be craving more, and I won't even have to ask. I knew that with a small nod, a pink pill would be in my hands. Just as if Michael did a sleight of hand trick. But unlike magic, the pills weren't an illusion. I couldn't just shake it off and call everything a trick. I had been down this path, and I knew where it led.

"Nah." I forced myself to stare straight at Michael's dark, triangular sunglasses. My own, clear reflection looked back at me and I was startled. I was still surprised to see my eyes without the red rims and deep circles. At rehab, I had to do what the counselors called, "The Mirror Exercise." In the exercise, we all had to look at ourselves in the mirror for at least a minute. It felt a bit strange to stare at my own face. The first time I looked in the mirror, it was like staring at a stranger, staring at someone who I'd forgotten existed. It reminded me of that poem the speaker gave us the first night in rehab. The one about getting what you wanted and then going to the mirror and asking that guy what he wanted. I was pretty sure the guy staring back at me didn't have a clue about too much of anything.

I looked at my reflection in Michael's sunglasses. I had a much better idea of what I wanted now. But it still felt like I was a newborn most of the time and learning to breathe again.

"Suit yourself." Michael shrugged and adjusted his sunglasses.

I had drawn a firm line in the sand. It was a line where I was standing on one side of the river and he was on the other. Michael wasn't any different than me. Both of us were diagnosed with Attention Deficit Disorder in third grade. Both of us self-medicated by the time we got to eighth grade with substances that weren't exactly legal. And both of us were addicts. The only difference was, I was ninety days down the road of sobriety ahead of him. But, one slip, and I would be back to where he was: believing a pill could give me courage and solutions to all my problems.

Just as I started thinking there might be something I could say to Michael, a shadow moved in the large, plate-glass office window behind him. It wasn't an accident he cornered me outside the main office. Michael was trying to trap me. The previous spring, I was the school's poster-boy for drugs. "Baseball star gets busted for drugs." The school's faculty and parent committee made sure the story hit the papers. They wanted everyone to know the newfound drug policy worked. Right out of the gate, I was snagged with a dirty UA.

Now clean and sober, everyone on the small campus was obviously watching me. I wasn't going to be able to do anything out of the ordinary. Probably right now, a phone call was being made to Mom. The secretary would quietly tell her Michael and I were observed engaged in a suspicious activity. Mom could easily insist I have another UA. Dad might have taken my side. He might have seen the truth. But Dad wasn't there. I knew the UA would come up clean, even though the last two days had made me want to use again. I managed to keep it clean. Last night I picked up Mom's wine glass, and thought about rubbing my tongue around the outside and bottom of the glass, just to suck up any leftover drops. But I didn't. It made me angry that no one trusted me without shoving a "Pee Here" cup under my nose.

I turned abruptly away from Michael and shaded my eyes against the morning sun. In the distance, McCallister was surrounded by a cluster of people. The morning was quickly steamrolling into a disaster, and I felt a small tightening in my chest. I needed to do something before things imploded on me.

Without saying another word to Michael, I headed in the direction of the milling group of people. McCallister already made her judgments against me. She saw me, last winter, all zoned out in her class. Other teachers sent me work to do in rehab. But McCallister handed me an "F," and told me to register for summer school. I got a long lecture from Mom and Dad about the cost of summer school, and how I should find a way to pay for it. Mom also tossed in an added lecture on the expense of rehab. She warned me I'd better not even think of relapsing because paying for a second time in rehab was out of the question. Dad tried to argue with her, but she shut him up with one look.

"He will stay sober," she insisted. "There is no money to pay for rehab a second or third time. He will do it right the first time."

A flying soccer ball hurled at me from the roof of the science wing. I dodged it and strode past a cluster of people with clipboards and stopwatches.

"Sorry I'm late," I said. "I lost track of time." I figured the best policy was honesty. There was no point in making excuses. I was pretty good at charming most of my teachers, and sometimes even Mom. But McCallister never fell for any charm. She had always been hardnosed and strict with me. Sometimes to the point of what I might even call biased and unfair. And I should know. I was lucky enough to get McCallister for biology and now physics—twice.

A soccer ball zinged past my ear, and a voice from the roof hollered down at us. "Sorry!" "What the—!" I jumped back as two more soccer balls rained down from the roof. How did McCallister get permission for this activity? Should I duck and cover before another set of balls showered me? McCallister grabbed my arm, and with a not so gentle push, guided me to the eaves under the building.

"Everyone is paired off," she said. Her voice hard and stern—as it usually was when she talked to me. I took a small step back and away from her because her breath smelled like it needed a big dose of clean-gum freshening.

"There's a gal up there who needs a partner." Jarrod tapped me on the arm as he recorded the time of one of the balls onto a clipboard. His curly blonde hair bobbed on his head. "She's a science champion."

"Science fair champion." My ears perked up. The girl had to be smart. She probably didn't know anyone if she was from the other high school. She was up there just waiting for someone to be her partner.

"Thanks for the tip," I said. Jarrod was the first baseman on the baseball team. He helped cover for me a lot during my using days. He'd tell the coaches I wasn't feeling well, or I'd had a long night studying. At rehab, they called Jarrod an enabler—someone who lied for the addict. It all seemed pretty harmless to me, but the counselors said if Jarrod hadn't lied maybe the coaches would have figured out what was going on sooner. I was pretty sure the coaches knew what was going on, and no one wanted to say anything. We could lose the championship without my pitching arm.

But now, I was just grateful to have Jarrod's support. I was worried about coming back to school and being treated like someone from another planet, and really, I was the same guy. I was just sober. I swallowed hard and asked Jarrod, "Do you know who it is?"

There weren't a lot of girls in summer physics. Marissa was supposed to be in this class, too. Marissa was Michael's girlfriend. She missed as much school as Michael and I. Marissa wasn't dumb. She was smart, except when it came to Michael, and then it seemed like I was always helping her out of one jam or another. I figured if we ended up lab partners, I was going to be doing a lot of counseling about Michael which was not appealing at all.

"The girl goes to the public high school," Jarrod said. "It's good to see you back."

"Yea," I said. "It's good to be back." Before McCallister could disagree with me about picking my own lab partner, I yanked open the door, and took the steps two at a time. I arrived on the black asphalt roof.

Immediately, I saw her.

Sarah.

It was my lucky day. It would be easy to slide up next to her and suggest we be partners. I was always good with the girls. Always had more than my share to choose from. Of course, that was all when I was using. Everyone said it was going to be different now I was sober. They said I would have to relearn how to be around girls again, and the feelings could make me want to use again. I figured I'd take my chances. I stuck my hands into my pockets and, in what I hoped, was a casually stride, I glided forward. "Surprise you?" I said as I tapped Sarah's shoulder.

I leaned back on my heels and took in her red sandals. I was immediately in love with her red-painted toe nails. I loved when girls painted their toenails. I couldn't explain why. But I loved it. I knew enough about girls to realize Sarah put some thought into her outfit. She was wearing a flowered skirt and crisp white t-shirt. It sure wasn't what the girls around here wore. Most of them wore shorts and t-shirts and looked like they could care less about dressing for summer school. Except for Marissa, who waved lazily at me from her spot on the left side of the roof. Marissa always looked like she was going to a party and pretty much wore the same type of clothes. Tight cropped pants and low cut shirts. I nodded in her direction.

"I've got to talk to you," Marissa yelled, but before she could move, Jarrod hollered from below.

"Throw the ball, Marissa."

She glared at him, and then hurled the ball high in the air. "Later," she mouthed before she turned around and leaned so far over the roof I was a little afraid she was going to fall.

But before I could rush to help Marissa, Sarah shoved a soccer ball in my hands. "Here. I'm going to the ground."

"What if I want to be on the ground?" I said with what I hoped was a lot of charm. There seemed to be a lot of activity on the roof McCallister didn't have a clue about.

Sarah didn't answer. She stepped away, clutched her stomach and looked a little green. I took a step back and hoped she wasn't going to throw up. In school, whenever someone threw up, the janitors rushed around with that sawdust stuff and tossed it over the mess. Of course, it always made some other kid toss his cookies too.

And then with a large oompf, Sarah threw up. Everyone turned to watch, except Marissa. She was still leaning over the rooftop, and yelling at Jarrod not to be such a klutz and to catch the ball the next time. I was left wondering if this is what everyone meant when they said girls were going to be a challenge to my sobriety.

CHAPTER FIVE

Shantel

I leaned against the white, concrete wall in the stairwell. No one threw up in high school— especially not the first day at a new school, and not in front of someone you wanted to impress. My footsteps dragged as I made my way downstairs. The last time I threw up in front of anyone was…no. No. I shook my head. I did not want to go there. It didn't matter. It didn't matter when the last time was that I threw up. I threw up today. The inside of my mouth tasted like this morning's oatmeal and toast; if there was anything left in my stomach, it would have come up too.

After I'd gotten off the phone with Drew this morning, I'd been surprised to see that Dad fixed breakfast. I usually just ate a granola bar or yogurt bar on the bus to school. I was the first one to be picked up, which meant the bus ride was forty-minutes long every morning.

"I thought you could use a little something for your first day," Dad said and smiled at me.

"You need to keep your strength up to learn all you can."

I'd sat down in the chair he held out, and discovered I was hungry. Oatmeal and toast was a lot better than the cold breakfast bars.

Now, I held my stomach, and prayed nothing would surge upward. I was pretty sure I'd gotten sick because of the height. When Mrs. McCallister told us part of the lab involved throwing balls from a place on the school's one story roof, I'd felt my stomach roll.

I've never been a fan of heights and avoided them at all costs. One time, Dad bought tickets to the Space Needle to see the Fourth of July fireworks. I spent most of the night lying on the floor.

Gingerly, I had climbed the stairs to the roof. Mrs. McCallister wanted us to look down at the ground for some last minute instructions. That was when things started to go wrong. I could see Mrs. McCallister, and I could see the tops of five or six heads, and then everything started to spin. By the time I looked up, Christopher was there. And instead of making me feel better, seeing him made my vision whirl even more.

And the next thing I knew....Well, it wasn't a pretty picture. The same as....Again, I stopped myself. I will not remember. I will not remember. I chanted the mantra as I exited the stairwell and stepped onto the ground.

"Is everything okay?" Mrs. McCallister asked. "You look a little pale."

I wanted to say of course everything was not okay. I had no partner for the lab because everyone knew each other, and I hated heights. Then, just when I thought I might have someone as my lab partner, and even better, it turned out to be Christopher, I had to go and throw up. No, everything was not okay. But that was not what Mrs. McCallister wanted to hear, and it was not what I was programmed to tell her. So, I lied, and said that yes, of course everything was okay.

Christopher yelled from the roof. "Where is my partner?"

I smiled at Mrs. McCallister, and, holding the clipboard in front of my chest, walked over to a spot where I could look up at him.

Christopher stood on the edge and grinned down at me. "Here you go," he called as a ball careered toward me.

"Wait," I yelled and ducked from the flying ball. "I don't have the timer set up." I fumbled for the watch and score sheet. At this rate, we were going to fail the assignment. And suddenly, that made me want to be sick again.

"Come on, Superstar," Christopher called. "Get it

together."

Get it together. I grimaced. I had just hurled, and he was telling me to "get it together?" I raised my face toward the roof and glared at him. "Send the next ball down," I hollered. I'd show him just how together I could be.

But, as another ball flew past me, and I missed the score, I knew getting it together was not going to be easy.

Christopher yelled, "Did you get that one?" "No," I shouted. "Try again."

Christopher leaned over and scooped up a ball out of the bin on the roof. He took a step back, wound his arm behind his head, and then released the ball. The ball moved towards me, but instead of recording the speed, I found myself watching Christopher's muscles. I marveled at how effortlessly he could toss the ball. All of his muscles moved together in one synchronized movement.

The ball sailed over me, but when I looked at Christopher, he was grinning at me with that sexy, lazy grin I'd seen in the theater's street fair booth. And then, I knew he was doing it on purpose. He was making sure I couldn't catch the ball, showing off by tossing the ball like he would on the baseball field. Christopher was flirting with me. I grinned back at him. "Wanna try again?" I asked in what I hoped was a sexy voice. I didn't care how long it took for us to do the lab.

The next thirty minutes passed quickly, as Christopher showed off his pitching arm, and I missed every ball's speeding time.

On purpose.

I'd never had so much fun playing catch and miss.

But when Mrs. McCallister called time and asked for the lab sheets, I glanced down at our blank one with horror. We wasted the entire class. We'd flunk the lab.

I didn't have time to think.

I quickly walked up to the boy who had been catching balls next to me. I'd heard his lab partner call him Jarrod, and without hesitating, I explained to Jarrod how I'd been sick, and just hadn't been able to get the right times recorded for the ball tosses. I told him I was new and it had all been a little much the first day.

Jarrod looked at me for a minute before he spoke. "Chris is a friend of mine. Here you go."

I jotted down his times onto my paper before I walked over to Mrs. McCallister. I explained we didn't have enough time to do the math equations. I told her how I'd gotten a little sick on the roof, and that it took me awhile to get a hang of recording the times. I figured if I had to be embarrassed, then I might as well make the most of it. I was never one of those girls who used illness as a way to get out of gym, but now, it seemed like a little illness could work in my favor.

Mrs. McCallister studied me and I squirmed under her gaze. I knew she didn't believe me. But, I also knew she wanted more than anything to be a part of the faculty at Dad's college. Dad was the head of his department, and Mrs. McCallister saw me as a way to get the position she coveted. I knew I was using that fact to my advantage, but right now, it was more important I didn't flunk the lab.

"Turn it in tomorrow," Mrs. McCallister said slowly before turning away from me to respond to someone else's question. "Just this once."

"Thank you." I gathered up my purse and books. I'd been given a reprieve, and I knew it.

"I'm hungry," Christopher said as he stepped up beside me. "Want to get lunch? Finish up this lab?" He peered at me from under his thick blond hair which hung almost to his eyes. "Unless..." Christopher stopped. "Well, unless you don't feel well. Then, we could just hang out here or something."

"I'm fine," I said brightly. "I would love lunch. A big lunch."

It didn't matter I was supposed to be in the literature class. I could skip it.

"Great," Christopher said. "I'll drive." He reached into his pocket and pulled out a set of car keys. "Where do you want to go?"

"The bakery? Mia always makes good sandwiches." I

didn't worry about Mia telling Dad I was skipping class. She didn't know my summer school schedule.

"No problem." Christopher turned and strode two steps ahead of me. I hurried after him and tried to keep up with his long strides. By the time we reached his truck in the parking lot, I was breathless. I prayed my armpits didn't have big sweat marks.

Christopher didn't seem to notice my panting as he slipped in the driver's side, and leaned over to unlock the passenger door. I placed my purse and book on the seat, and tried to hoist myself up. It took two tries before I was in the truck with the door shut behind me.

Christopher looked over and smiled at me. "It's kinda high, huh?"

"Yes," I said as I tried to discreetly wipe my sweating palms on my skirt. Christopher's spicy guy smell rose around me and made me a bit light headed.

Christopher started the truck and eased out of the parking lot. I stared straight ahead, and willed myself not to turn and look back at the school. Surely, no one would call Dad and tell him I wasn't there. It wasn't like regular school. It was summer school. And if they did, and Dad asked, I'd just tell him I got sick. That was the truth. I did get sick on the roof.

The bakery was only a few blocks away and, before I knew it, Christopher turned into the small parking lot behind the bakery. His fingers caressed the steering wheel and I couldn't help but think what his long slender fingers would feel like cupping my chin, pointing my face up to his, and then....

As soon as the truck stopped, I was overwhelmed with the need for fresh air. I was drowning in his scent, and my romantic visions. When I opened the truck door, it crashed against the wall, and I saw there was no room for me to get out.

Christopher swung his door open. "Mine opens fine." His eyes danced as he held out his hand. "Come on. Slide over."

I slipped my hand into Christopher's strong, warm hand. The truck seats were bench, so it was easy for me to slide into the driver's seat. I eased past the steering wheel and out of the truck. On the ground, we stood face to face. The space between us was nonexistent. Christopher's body pressed against mine as he wrapped his arms around me. "Hey there," he said softly. "Glad you feel better."

"Hey," I mumbled against his solid chest where I could have easily rested my head. I felt him rest his chin on the top of my head, but only for a moment before he slowly released me, and I wasn't even sure if the moment happened.

"The bakery is this way." I stepped around him and walked to the back door. My heart pounded as I pulled open the heavy wood service door. Did Christopher really mean to hold me in his arms? Or was he just friendly and I was reading too much into it? As soon as I stepped into the building, I stopped and inhaled the warm aroma of bread, cookies, and coffee. Christopher was right behind me. When I halted, he bumped into me. I tried not to gasp as he pressed into me like we were a pair of spoons. His arms reached around me. His hands moved up and down my arms in a gentle caress. It was the second time Christopher held me in less than two minutes, and I was beginning to think I could really get used to it.

But just as I was dreaming I could stay all day, wrapped in Christopher's arms, Mia peered around a large silver stove. Her long hair was caught up in a tight bun that looked like a spider's web around her hair. "Sorry! I didn't know you were busy."

I blushed and stepped away from Christopher. "Hey, Mia," I said as I stepped forward and tried to act like nothing out of the usual had happened. I pretended having a warm male body pressed next to me, in the back of a hot bakery, happened every day.

Mia winked at me and shoved a tray of unpainted blue moon sugar cookies into the oven. "Flip the Closed sign," Mia said. "I'll make some sandwiches. It's been a slow morning." Mia closed the oven and then leaned forward. She smiled at Christopher. "And who are you?"

"Christopher," I called over my shoulder. I headed toward the front door, turned the small gold lock, and flipped the hand-woven sign. I prayed Mia didn't bring up the eighth grade dance. I blushed as I remembered how it had taken her all night, plus a shot of something that made my insides feel all warm, to calm me down.

"Nice to see you again," Mia said smoothly.

I quickly hopped over to the refrigerator and opened the door. As the wave of cool air hit me, I wished I could step inside. I was on fire. Instead, I pulled out two bottled waters as Mia stepped up beside me.

"You okay with this?" she whispered.

"I'll be fine," I whispered back. I tried to appear nonchalant.

"He turned out pretty good-looking," Mia said.

"He's my lab partner."

"Physics?" She grinned. "The two of you coming through the back door looked like chemistry to me."

The heat moved into my face and I turned away from Mia. I didn't want Christopher to overhear us talking. I casually headed back towards Christopher. "Water?" I asked when I reached the table.

"Thanks, Sarah," Christopher leaned back in his chair, crossed his legs at the ankle and opened the water bottle. His eyes never left my face.

I squirmed. He'd just called me Sarah again. Who was Sarah? Mia looked up from buttering a thick piece of bread and raised an eyebrow. I looked away. I had to tell him my name was Shantel. I had to tell him before Mia said anything. And by the way Mia's mouth opened slightly, I was pretty sure, any moment, she'd plunk down the sandwich and tell Christopher he'd better figure out how to call me by my name.

Slowly, I sat down next to Christopher and dug into my bag for my physics packet. Once it was on the table, I ran my fingers over the pages to smooth the creases. The numbers and problems swam before me. I frowned. Dad didn't mention what level of math class I should be in to take physics. But, I was pretty sure the math was higher than the Algebra II class I finished last year.

"Not too hard, Sarah," Christopher said as he tapped the

page in front of me.

Behind me, Mia cleared her throat. Loudly. "Shantel," I said slowly. The words felt funny on my lips. It was as if I was hearing my name for the first time.

"Who?" Christopher swung around and looked toward the door.

My name is Shantel, I said to myself. Why didn't he remember my name?

Christopher snapped his fingers. "We were in middle-school history, right?"

"French," I said softly. "French class." I stared at the table and studied the fingerprints on the glass topped table. When I was in kindergarten, we had a drawing class where we got to press our fingers in black dye, and then press the fingerprint to the page. Once we had a row of fingerprints, we had drawn legs, arms, eyes and mouths on them so the page came alive with happy characters. That picture hung on the refrigerator until I won my first blue ribbon in science.

I ran my fingers along the glass and over the smudged fingerprints. None of this was turning out the way I'd thought. We were supposed to be laughing. But, I didn't feel like laughing. I felt funny. As if something was lodged in my chest and I couldn't quite get it unstuck.

"French!" Christopher slapped the table. "Right! I remember!"

I peeked up at him, and as my eyes met his, I looked away. I stared down at the math problems and tried to concentrate. But all I could think about was Christopher and the funny feeling inside me.

"Look," Christopher said softly. "It's just I was kinda messed up then. I wouldn't have forgotten your name. I remember you."

"You do?" I slowly raised my eyes to his. I wanted to believe him. I wanted to believe he did remember me. It was just a little mistake. Christopher didn't remember me the way I remembered him. But what did eighth grade French really matter? That was two years ago. We were different now.

"I do." He gently took my hand and wove his fingers through mine. I stared at them linked together. Did Christopher really remember me?

CHAPTER SIX

Christopher

I felt bad about messing up Shantel's name. And the thing was; I did remember her. It took me a while, because well, we weren't in eighth grade anymore. She didn't look at all like she did in eighth grade. Shantel used to be bony thin. Now, when I held her in my arms, well, I kinda went all squirmy inside. She had curves and more curves. But, the name thing was just another place where my addict was trying to trip me up. Remind me it wasn't so long ago when he was in control. I know he can take charge real fast again. So I have to play it smooth.

I watched Shantel out of the corner of my eye. She was a Science Fair Champion and I expected her to fly through the equations. I purposely delayed starting my own work, so she could tease me and ask when I would be finished. I picked up my pencil and absently tapped it against the bakery table. Even though McCallister seemed to think I spent my entire Junior year stoned, especially in her class, I paid attention to some of what she said. This lab was a repeat of one we did last October. The only difference was, last October we filed into the computer lab and threw computerized balls. I liked the outdoor lab better.

Shantel was always smarter than me in French. She was in all the high achiever classes. Just like the physics summer class. Unlike me, Shantel was there to get some extra class work on her transcript. I probably could have been in high achiever classes myself if my "other recreational activities" hadn't taken the place of homework.

But Shantel wasn't gloating, or getting finished first and wondering why I wasn't done yet. Instead, small bits of pink eraser covered the table and she had erased every number on the page. Her knuckles whitened as she gripped her pencil, her face twisted into a funny grimace.

It seemed to me Shantel was pretty agitated and I didn't want to interrupt her intense scribbles. I didn't always pick up the best clues from girls, but this time, I could tell that now was not the time to tease her. Instead, I quickly jotted down some answers to my equations, and then listened to Gloria and Mia, whose voices drifted over in snatches of conversation. Gloria came in the back door about five minutes ago. She's the Children's Theater director who was in the street fair booth with Shantel. I hoped she wouldn't mention the broken mosaic pieces.

"….not enough shows…" "…donations are down…"

"...need the annual fund raiser to count…"

Gloria slammed her hand on the counter. I jumped and she looked over. "Sorry." Her lips formed the word silently.

I was glad to see Mia focused on something beside me. Mia had been watching us like she was ready to swoop in and rescue her baby chick. She seemed to resent me, but for the life of me, I couldn't figure out why. Shantel and I never went out. It's not like I did something to hurt the girl. The only thing I could think of was it must have something to do with the eighth grade dance. But, that was never a date. My date was Michael and his pills.

I twirled my pencil and looked around the bakery. Colorful posters covered the walls. They showcased every performance at the Children's Theater. It was actually a unique decorating scheme instead of something like boring pale peach paint. I searched for one about Dad's magic shows. When I was younger, I often went to practice with him. My favorite part of practice was the lighting. Each swing of stage lights sent arcs of white beams across the floor revealing etched tape pieces and large scratches.

Below the stage was an orchestra pit that hadn't been used in years. Gloria used the pit for cast off pieces of costumes, scarves, wigs, gloves, and old broken set pieces.

I loved the orchestra pit. The stage junk yard, Gloria called it. But to me, the pit was far more than just a stage junk yard. The orchestra pit was my magic playground. The place where I could pretend to be anyone I wanted. I spent hours dressing in wigs, hats, and hunting for just the right prop that had been tossed aside in a hurry by some actor or actress.

But the most interesting part of the orchestra pit was Alexandra, the stage pit ghost. I first met Alexandra when I was hunting for a top hat. The old wigs and clothes to the left of me moved of their own accord. I was pretty sure I hadn't touched the clothes. That's when Alexandra rose in a misty form, out of the stack of clothes. Gloria always said every good theater had a ghost. Most people around town assumed the resident theater ghost was pretty much only a legend— something to draw in the locals for the annual Halloween Theater ghost tours. But I knew ghosts really existed.

Alexandra perched on top of a toy chest. "You're a ghost." I wasn't scared. Instead, I was relieved to have someone in the pit with me. I didn't ever want to admit it. But sometimes, waiting for Dad to finish a show got lonely. Now, I had a friend.

"I am a ghost," Alexandra said. "And you're human."

I'd spent the afternoon with Alexandra, and when Dad finished, I expected him to be able to see the ghost too. But instead, he leaned down, looked me directly in the eye, and said, "It doesn't matter if I see the ghost, son. The important thing is you do. Magic is about believing in things we can't see. It's about the illusion we create for others to believe."

Now, I wondered what type of magic I had to believe in to release Dad from jail. The bail was high, and Mom wasn't budging an inch about getting him out.

"He's going to stay there until the sentencing," she said when I asked. "He knows why." And that was the end of the conversation.

I wasn't sure I still believed in ghosts, but I did believe in magic. I believed magic could make you forget everything that was bothering you. I believed magic sometimes came wrapped up in small pills, and sometimes wrapped up in bottles. And now, I was just starting to learn how to believe in the magic that came from being sober. I stared at Shantel. What did she believe in?

As if she felt my stare, Shantel looked up, and our eyes met. For a minute, I was lost in the pools of her hazel eyes. I could drown in her hazel eyes. And then, she looked away, and I was left with an insatiable urge. It was like a drug rush, without the drug. Notice me. Notice me. Notice me, my addict brain pleaded, and I listened because after all it wasn't a drug I craved, it was Shantel. And that had to be better than a drug.

I lined my pencil up next to my nostril, and covered my other nostril with my left hand. Slowly, I began to work the pencil up my nose. The trick was that I kept it covered with my right hand and then slipped the pencil into my shirt pocket. It was an old trick. But, it always made people laugh. The conversation with Mia and Gloria intensified. It seemed like the whole bakery could use a little bit of a humor.

I'd barely started to slip the imaginary pencil into my nose before Mia nudged Gloria. Small smiles played around the corners of their lips. I winked at them and continued to push what looked like the pencil into my nose. Slowly, I moved my left foot and nudged Shantel's small foot under the table.

Shantel frowned, and looked up at me. Her eyes widened in surprise.

I raised my eyebrows at her, and then, very carefully, removed both hands and turned them palm side up. By all appearances, I have shoved the pencil into my nose. But, the pencil is still tucked in my shirt pocket. That was the genius of the trick.

Magic.

Mia tossed back her head and laughed. Gloria smiled.

But, Shantel only stared coldly at me. "What are you doing?"

"A little magic." I shrugged as if it was no big deal. But I couldn't keep the hope out of my voice. "Like it?"

"It's…" Shantel struggled for composure. "It's…"

"Yes?"

"Childish." Shantel turned away from me and back to the math problems.

The pencil dropped out of my sleeve and crashed to the floor. Behind me, Gloria and Mia clapped loudly.

Childish? Magic is childish? When did Shantel become so jaded? I thought she liked magic. Everyone likes magic.

I was stunned. I leaned over to pick up the pencil. How could Shantel not like a magic trick? Hadn't she heard of people like David Copperfield, David Blaine, and Houdini? Those guys drew in millions with their shows. There was nothing childish about them. Okay, so the pencil trick wasn't David Copperfield, but magic was magic. She should have been enthralled. She should have been hanging onto my every word, and pleading for another trick. Instead, she wasn't interested at all.

She erased and scratched out math problems like she was trying to erase something far deeper and more wrong than any math problem.

"That was great," Gloria exclaimed.

"We loved it," Mia said.

"Thanks," I said modestly as I peeked at Shantel out of the corner of my eye. She was watching me out of the corner of her eye. As soon as our eyes meet, both of us looked away. I couldn't help smiling. She was listening.

Gloria returned to talking about the theater and the annual show. Suddenly, I knew how to impress Shantel.

"I heard you talking," I said to Gloria. I leaned back in my chair, and acted like it wasn't a big deal. I crossed my hands over my head. "Do you need another performer? For that special show you were talking about?" I would pack the house with my performance. Shantel would be swept away.

"Of course," Gloria exclaimed. Her expression brightened. "Why didn't we think of it? You can do magic! Like your father." Suddenly her face darkened, as if she just remembered the three-ring circus going on with Dad right now.

I let the legs of the chair crash to the ground, all four on the floor. I felt nauseous. Why didn't I think before I spoke? The counselors and teachers have been telling me that since I was in second grade. "If you'd just think through what you're going to do, you might not find yourself in so much trouble." Of course, I never listened. Impulsivity is part of my disease. I want what I want, now. And the worst thing was, Shantel didn't even notice. She just kept scratching out numbers.

CHAPTER SEVEN

Shantel

When Mia dropped me off, the first thing I did was check the phone messages. There were two. The first, from someone named Betty at Cascadia and she wanted to know why I was not in Advanced Literature. I erased her message, and played the next. Someone by the name of Mrs. Smoot wanted me to be sure and check my e-mail. She sent the day's literature assignment, and hoped I'd be in class tomorrow. I erased that one too, and sat down at the computer to check my e-mail. I have access to Dad's e-mail too. He never checks it, so I did a quick check of his account and found a message from the same Betty asking about my attendance. I deleted it. Sorry, Betty. We didn't get the message. I will be in class tomorrow, and everything will be fine. I printed off the literature assignment. We are to read Beauty and the Beast and then chose one character that is most like us, and write a reflective essay on the character. I smiled. This one would be easy.

There was a manila folder by Dad's computer, with a couple more invoices tossed inside. I opened it and scanned the sales from the past weekend's Markets. Jam and strawberries were selling well. There was also an invoice which demanded payment. I frowned, and clicked into the farm's monthly spread sheet. Our booth hasn't been paid for. I grabbed the checkbook and wrote a check from the farm account. By the time the check cleared, we would have deposited money from the jam and berries. It should cover it.

This time.

I replaced the folder, and headed toward my room. My brain felt tight. It was too much. We were barely holding on, and the letter still tucked in my purse was further verification of that fact.

I had to tell Dad. But, there was nothing he could do. He didn't know how bad it was. I kept it from him. He didn't ask, and I didn't tell. Both of us played our own little game of pretend. Sometimes I wondered how things would be different if we'd had the life insurance policy. But it was no use saying "if." The facts were we didn't.

In my room, I sat down at the loom, and picked up the warp. There was one place that still soothed me. One place I could go and find order—weaving. My cell phone beeped. It was Drew sending me another text message.

After Christopher had left the bakery, I'd gone down to the coffee shop and used book store where I always meet Drew. This summer, he was working in the bookstore, and I found him with his head buried in a box of old books.

"Aren't these great?" he asked as soon as he saw me. Drew held up an old set of Shakespeare books. Usually, I would have sat with him as he went through the old books which came in when people cleaned out attics or basements, but today, I felt restless and unsettled. The last thing I wanted to do was go through a box of old books. He wanted to know everything about class, and when I'd told him we really hadn't done much but a lab where we threw balls from the roof, Drew insisted he'd text me later to find out "all the details."

Now, I ignored his text plea for "all the details."

There was a loud crack under my feet. Thinking about Drew caused me to put too much pressure on the pedal, and something broke. Sometimes I think Karma has a strange way of playing games with you

I dropped to the red, blue, and yellow Persian carpet in my bedroom. The broken treadle lay at an angle under the loom. It was all I could do not to burst out crying. Everything seemed to be going wrong.

I peered up at the tangled lavender and cream wool scarf on the loom. It would take me just as long to untangle the yarn and re-warp the loom as it would to start the whole project over. Frustrated, I tried to see where the treadle had cracked. Was there a bolt I could re-attach to the loom?

A couple months ago, I'd seen the loom posted for sale at the bakery. Mia keeps a bulletin board on the back wall where people post flyers for sales, lost and found, and work-for-hire. I was sweeping the floor and the bright yellow flyer caught my eye. The flyer hadn't been there the day before, and I was excited to see a family heirloom floor loom was for sale. I borrowed money from Mia with the promise I'd work extra time at the bakery. Now, I wasn't sure where I'd ever find that extra time. After I called and got the address, Mia drove me over. The loom was in pretty bad shape. Mia took one look, and told me I'd be lucky to get one scarf out of it.

I'd been lucky….until now.

In the driveway, a car door slammed.

Startled, I stood and tried to peek out the window. No one came to visit on the farm—not this late. I hurried down the darkened hallway to the stairs.

In the living room, I pushed back the thin lace curtains and attempted to make out who was here. Before I could see much, the doorbell rang. It wasn't Mia or Grandma and Grandpa. Mia always walked directly into the house. She would sing out, "Anyone home?" Grandma and Grandpa knocked and then walked right in. "We knew you were home," they'd say. "We didn't want to give you time to straighten up." Which always made Dad and me laugh because we both knew it would take more than Grandma and Grandpa's visits for Dad to pick up his stacks of papers lying haphazardly around the room.

The only other person who sometimes stopped by the farm was Drew. But I'd already seen him this afternoon. Although he would text me a hundred times, he wasn't likely to drop by too.

The doorbell rang again, and I stepped away from the

curtains. I unlatched the front door and stared into Christopher's blue eyes.

"Hey, Shantel," Christopher said as he leaned against the door frame. He smiled lazily at me and I melted.

"Hey," I mumbled. I clutched the door handle and tried to hold onto my swirling emotions. We hadn't left the bakery on the best terms. I hoped Christopher would do the math problems, and then I could ask to see them. Instead, he did nothing but talk about magic. And magic made me remember. Even now, as I stood at the door, the memories swirled around me and I tightened my grip on the wood.

A magician came to perform for the children's unit of the hospital when Mom was ill. The nurses thought a magic show might be something I would enjoy. I wanted to tell them I wasn't seven. But, seeing the haggard and strained look on Dad's face, and taking the gentle nudge from Mia, I knew I didn't have a choice. So, I reluctantly followed the nurse down the hall to the elevator.

Unfortunately, the Magician chose me as his audience member favorite. I tried to be surprised when he pulled a coin out of my ear, and then an Ace of Spades card. However, when, the Magician tried to convince me to be the girl he "sawed in half," I lost my patience. I flipped open the box to reveal the secret space inside—the secret to his trick. The nurses quickly ushered me away from the crying children, but the damage was done. I knew I should have felt bad, but I didn't. I wanted someone to take away the pain inside.

"You left this," Christopher held up my silver watch bracelet, "in the truck."

Automatically, my hand flew to my bare wrist. My watch bracelet. How could I not have noticed it was gone? Something inside me felt terrible. My chest contracted and everything around me got a little fuzzy before I swallowed hard and reached out to take the bracelet. My fingers brushed over Christopher's long, slender ones.

"Let me get that." Christopher gently took my left arm. When his fingers touched my wrist, my insides tingled and the warmth spread through me. Above us, a wind chime tinkled in a small gust of wind. I caught my breath as the musical notes floated across the porch.

A memory played in the corners of my mind. It was another good day and Mom stood on a small step stool. She hung the chime on the small white eye-hook. The chime caught the wind, and Mom pulled me close to her. "It's beautiful," she said. "Just like you." I snuggled closer to her. I wanted to believe her words. But it was hard at age twelve; with my long, spindly legs, and flat chest, I didn't feel beautiful. Not like Mom, with her round face, dark sparkling eyes, and her wonderful laugh. When she laughed it always sounded like her own musical chimes.

Christopher placed the bracelet on my arm, and a small breeze whispered through the porch and across my face. Christopher's eyes met mine, and his fingers lightly caressed my hand. The world seemed to stand still for just a minute. A minute that held the two of us captured in a small bubble which seemed like it might be one of those quantum shifts of time—until a large flock of Canada geese, flying overhead, honked loudly.

"Would you like to come inside?" I leaned against the door for balance. It was funny how just those simple words made me feel so out of balance.

"Nice place," Christopher said as he stepped inside and looked around.

I wasn't sure it was such a nice place. It was a messy place. Dad's books and papers were always tossed everywhere, and I didn't know the last time anyone dusted. A water glass sat on the wood coffee table without a coaster, next to a plate that still held chocolate cake crumbs. Thick oriental carpets covered the hardwood floor, and if you didn't look too closely, you couldn't see the dirt caked into the swirls and patterns of the red and blue rugs. But Christopher wasn't looking at any of those things. Instead, he was standing in front of the large picture window which overlooked the farm.

"It's better upstairs," I said. "The best view is the one from my window."

"Really?" Christopher turned and smiled lazily at me with that same look in his eyes I'd seen in the doorway.

I flushed. I just invited Christopher upstairs—to my bedroom. The heat rose higher in my face. I tried to cover my nervousness, "The treadle on my loom. It broke. I don't know what to do. Maybe you can…"

"No problem," Christopher said as he strode toward the wood stairs. "I'll take a look."

"Okay," I mumbled. My heart was pounding. I barely touched ground as I followed behind him. Cleo scurried out of the living room and ran upstairs. I hoped Christopher liked cats.

"The room with the light?" Christopher asked as we reached the top of the stairs.

"Yes." I tried to think. I'd put away all my laundry, I made my bed, there wasn't anything lying out where it wasn't supposed to be. It should all be perfectly normal. If you could call having Christopher in my bedroom, when Dad wasn't home, perfectly normal.

Christopher was already squatting under my loom by the time I got into the room. I stood behind him and tried not to notice how his thick hair fell over his t-shirt collar, or the small row of freckles along the back of his neck.

"Got some bad news." He peered at the broken boards. "The board's cracked in two."

"What?" I asked, while I tried to pull myself away from counting his freckles.

"I can get some pieces of wood. See if I can fix it for you," Christopher said at the same time Cleo dashed into the yarn. In what looked like a comedy of errors, the cat went to the right and Christopher rolled to the left.

I tried hard not to laugh at the surprised look on his face. He lay sprawled on the floor with his arms going one way and his legs the other. I stepped closer to him and held out my hand. As his fingers slipped into mine, a warm feeling rushed through me.

"Gotcha, Superstar," Christopher said as he stood up beside me. He wrapped his arms around me the way he'd done in the bakery.

"Umpfh." Seemed the only word I could manage.

"Shantel," Christopher murmured.

"Mmmm." I enjoyed the way my name sounded on his lips.

Slowly, he began to rub small circles on my back before he reached up, and cupped my chin. Lifting my face, Christopher lowered his mouth to mine and time seemed to stop. Softly at first, we moved our lips, and then, hesitantly, I parted my mine just a bit. Christopher's tongue quickly moved inside my mouth and swirled gently. Christopher pressed his hands against my lower back and drew me closer to him.

Thinking fast about what the romance heroines did, I moved my fingers softly into his hair. The kiss deepened, and Christopher's hands moved slowly down my sides, and then up under my shirt. I knew I should tell him to stop. We were alone in my bedroom. Dad could come home at any minute. But a part of me didn't want him to stop. I wanted him to keep going. I wanted to see what happened.

Christopher's fingers played with the edges of my bra. "Want to take it off?" he murmured.

In a bit of a haze, I stepped away from Christopher. I lowered my hands to the edges of my t-shirt and then froze. What was I doing? Everything was moving so fast. So fast, I could barely think. Out of the corner of my eye, I saw myself in the mirror. My face was flushed. My shirt was askew, and I looked like I was terrified.

This wasn't how I was supposed to look. I was supposed to look like I was enjoying it. I looked like a fright show was happening.

I stepped away from Christopher and straightened my shirt. I combed my fingers through my hair and ran my tongue over my lips. But, I couldn't look at him. I was so confused. I wanted him to keep going. I wanted to see what it would be like to be with him. But it all seemed so out of control. And out of control was scary. When people got out of control, bad things happened. "Maybe later?" I muttered.

"Okay." Christopher adjusted his shirt. Without looking at me he said, "I should probably get going."

"Sure," I mumbled. My stomach cramped. Why did he want to leave now? We could have hung out like Drew and I. We could have talked about physics. But he wanted to leave. Did that mean I just blew my chance with him? Why didn't I let it go just a bit further? I was sure Christopher thought I was a baby for stopping. I was fifteen. Old enough not to get freaked out by a little kiss in my bedroom. I wanted to rush over to him, throw off my shirt, and tell him I'd made a mistake. Instead, I followed Christopher down the stairs and attempted to breathe normally. By the time we reached the living room, my stomach was so tight I thought I might throw up. Again.

Christopher leaned against the screen door. "See you in physics."

"Physics," I muttered. "Physics."

I shut the door slowly, turned, and headed back up the stairs. One of the family photos hanging on the stairway wall was crooked, and I stopped to straighten it. Mom perched on a small wooden stool. Dad stood behind her with his right hand lightly touching her shoulder. I leaned against Mom. My bangs were crooked because Mom tried to give me a quick haircut right before the photographer arrived. It hadn't been one of her good days, and she'd been in bed pretty much most of the morning. Finally, fifteen minutes before the photographer showed up, she crept downstairs. Her skirt was on at an angle, and her shirt wasn't pressed. Mom's dark eyes were wild and darted everywhere. She'd taken one look at me, grabbed the scissors from the kitchen cabinet, and then hauled me up on the kitchen stool. I'd been so afraid of her I hadn't moved an inch when she began cutting.

"Liz," Dad said. "I don't think you're—"

Mom stopped. Pointed the scissors at Dad and said, "Don't you dare tell me I can't cut my daughter's hair." Mom hadn't gotten very far before the photographer arrived. She tossed the scissors into the drawer, and yanked me off the stool. "Remember to smile," she'd said.

I rubbed my fingers over the heavy plate glass. The picture turned out okay, and no one had known anything. Mom's shirt wrinkles weren't visible, and her skirt draped around her. After the photographer left, Mom went back to bed, and Dad and I spent the rest of the night playing a card game and not talking about what happened.

By Christmas, Mom gushed about what a wonderful picture it was of all of us. Under Dad's directions, I framed the picture for her. It was an old silver frame I found in the back of the bakery. No one knew what had once been inside the frame. I took the frame home, painted it, and then slipped the family photo inside.

"That was Christopher," I said to the picture. I swallowed hard. A murky grey mist swarmed around me. Engulfed me. Threatened to drown me. But I couldn't stop it. I couldn't stop wondering how it would be if Mom were here right now. Would it be one of her bad days, or would it be one of her good days? If it was a good day, she would have asked me to grab a little bucket, slip on a pair of gloves, and help her in the garden. Mom would have given me the lecture about not letting things get too far out of hand. And I would have rolled my eyes and said, Mom! Sometimes, when I was at the mall, and saw girls arguing with their mom, I closed my eyes and pretended it was me standing there with Mom in the middle of the mall. We'd be arguing about why she wouldn't let me buy this or that.

I leaned against the stairwell wall. "Mom," I whispered.

The rising moon shone through the large round window above the stairs. When I was a child, I loved the moonlight nights. I'd awake to find the moon shining into my bedroom. I'd slip out of my bedroom and down the hall. Mom never woke once she went to bed, but Dad slept lightly, so I had to make sure the stairs didn't creak or the porch door slam. Once I'd made it into the barn, I loved to creep up to the loft and throw open the wide double doors. I'd make sure the hay was stacked below me before I'd slip one foot, and then one leg over the window ledge and perch myself on the edge. Looking down below, I never felt fear. Instead, I'd lean out into the darkness, and fall for what seemed like forever before I crashed into the hay with a soft plunk.

Over and over, I'd run up the loft ladder, and perch on the window ledge, before pushing myself off onto the hay below.

I was never scared.

CHAPTER EIGHT

Christopher

I pulled open the heavy, wood doors to the church and loped across the thin, orange carpet toward the basement. The dusty smell of churches used to make me sneeze, but now I'm used to it. I only smelled the coffee coming from the large pots. Those pots were always brewing at AA Meetings. If I got to the Meeting on-time, I had to walk through a small cluster of people having one last cigarette before heading inside. I often joked it was possible to find a Meeting anywhere. All I had to do was look for the smokers outside a church or community hall. Smoking is one thing I never picked up while I was using. As an athlete, I had enough sense to keep my lungs clear.

I slipped into the large room downstairs and looked for a metal folding chair in the back. I hadn't meant to stay so long with Shantel. But, once we got up to her room, and her hand slipped into mine.... It was like something came over me. Something I couldn't stop. I didn't know what to say to her afterward, so making an escape seemed like the easiest thing to do.

Charlie was sitting near the front of the room. He looked at me and then back to the speaker. I could guess what Charlie was thinking. Charlie told me I'm supposed to be at a Meeting every week. It's called my Home Group. That meant this Meeting was where my Sponsor attended on a regular basis and I was supposed to show up too. But, as Charlie was always saying, it wasn't enough to just show up. I had to do some service. Charlie kept pressing me to take on the role of Secretary or Chairperson of the Meeting. But the thought made my stomach queasy. I'd have to stand up front and open the Meeting with the words from the Big Book. I didn't have enough courage to do that yet. I never liked standing in front of people and reading. I flub words and mix up my sentences.

I attempted to get comfortable on the metal folding chair. At the podium, one of the old timers was talking about the importance of Sponsorship. I knew Sponsorship was important. It was why I had Charlie. They told us in treatment you had to get someone to help you work through the Twelve Steps. I thought it would be hard. But, when I walked into my first Meeting, Charlie assigned himself to me as my Sponsor. I wasn't sure that was how it always worked, but it seemed to work for us. In the front of the room, Charlie leaned forward, with his hands on his knees. He nodded at pretty much everything the old guy said.

I wasn't so enthralled with the Speaker. It all seemed the same to me. Get a Sponsor. Work the Steps. Be a Sponsor. I took a look around the room. I was easily the youngest person in the room by ten years. At treatment, we were all teens. I assumed the Meetings would have kids my age too. When the AA guys came out to the Treatment Center, they told us there were young people meetings. These were Meetings for people under twenty-five. In Seattle there are young people Meetings; in Riverview, it's pretty much the old guys and me.

The other thing about this Meeting was that it was always men. I asked Charlie about it. He said there was a Woman's Meeting at the same time, but in a different place. Charlie said most of the women wanted their own Meeting so they could talk about women stuff. Charlie said this was good so we could keep ourselves free of distractions. Everyone worried about distractions with the opposite sex at Meetings. I wasn't quite sure I had figured out why. I had heard married couples speaking together. They seemed very happy. But, I also heard guys who were miserable over some gal they'd met in a Meeting. I always chuckled to myself. It sounded so much like high school to me.

The Speaker stepped down from the podium and it was time for open sharing. Immediately, George started talking about his resentments with his ex-wife. It was the same every week. At first, I tried to pay attention. I thought I could learn something about staying sober and ex-wives. But after a couple weeks, I gave up. What did I need to know about ex-wives? I liked to date a lot of different girls. Or at least I had when I was using. I wasn't quite sure how it would go when I didn't have my magic pill to help me feel comfortable. And if what happened with Shantel was any indication, I could be in trouble.

I heard the whoosh of a hose being turned on and swung around to look out the basement sliding glass door. A church volunteer was watering a small garden of flowering plants. Dad loved blueberry plants. Blueberry plants line the property dividing line between our house and the Gibb's house. Dad and Tom Gibbs planted them one summer. I've been watering them every morning since Dad got arrested.

I shifted in my chair. The metal contraptions really got uncomfortable and I wished we had seat cushions. I was beginning to build resentments about Dad. Why is he in jail? Why is Mom so prickly about it? It was something I should talk about with Charlie. The old timers said things build up until, one day, you're drinking again. But, thinking about it was like poking tender bruises. Touch too hard and I would howl in pain.

"…close in the usual manner," the Meeting Chairperson intoned. Metal chairs scraped across the floor and jolted me out of my thoughts about Dad.

The closing prayer had barely ended before Charlie appeared at my side.

"Glad you could make it," he said in his soft voice. Charlie once lived in the South, and I could still hear the accent sometimes.

"I got caught up," I said, "helping someone." Charlie would understand helping someone. Wasn't that what he did for me as my Sponsor? Every time I saw Charlie, he was helping out somebody in AA. He was always working on somebody's house or talking to someone who was trying to get sober. Charlie went to a Meeting every day. AA is his life. I asked him and he said, "That's how it's done. You help others. And the helping of others helps you stay clean."

"Where is he?" Charlie took a quick look around the room. His dark eyes darted everywhere and missed nothing. "Did you bring him to the Meeting?"

"She's at her house." I knew immediately I said the wrong thing.

Charlie eyed me for a full minute. His dark stare was hard and direct. I squirmed under his gaze. I was supposed to be honest. But often, the honesty with Charlie made me wish I had a throw-up bucket nearby. I don't know how he learned to see through me, but whenever he gave me one of his looks, I felt like he could see every lie I've ever told.

"Careful, Christopher."

"Don't worry," I said. It was what I told everyone. When I felt like everything was about to knock down around me like a stack of dominoes, I always said, 'Don't worry'. It meant I had it all under control.

I didn't fool Charlie and he shook his head at me. "You want to stay sober," he said. "Stay away from the girls."

CHAPTER NINE

Shantel

I read the article carefully on my laptop while keeping an eye out for Mrs. McCallister to ask why I wasn't working on the research project in the early morning hours when I'd requested to use the physics classroom.

STAR HIGH SCHOOL BASEBALL PLAYER FAILS NEW DRUG POLICY.

Christopher Parks, junior varsity player, tested positive to the first urine analysis (UA) administered by Cascadia. Coach Williams says, "Christopher has always been one of our best players. We hope this will get him the help he needs." No mention was made as to whether Christopher will be returning to the team or not.

My stomach felt funny. I learned about drug use in health class. I knew all the facts. I knew about the statistics of families with addictions. I knew the signs to look for in friends and family. I knew all of it. But in health class, no one ever mentioned what happened if the guy you liked was one of the statistics. No one told us about the human factor. It reminded me of the fairytale I was supposed to be writing a paper about, Beauty and her Beast. Addicts were kinda like beasts to some people.

I studied the words carefully and looked for hints. Was this what Christopher meant when he said he was "messed up" and couldn't remember my name? After the eighth grade dance, the only thing anyone could talk about was how Christopher had been taken away in a police car. The rumors buzzed with the news that Christopher got caught with drugs. But I couldn't believe it. There had to be a mistake of some sort. We'd hear about it by the time we got back to school in the fall. But, when school started again, Christopher was gone. I kept asking if anyone knew what happened to him, and finally, someone said they heard he was transferred to Cascadia.

But, it did explain why Christopher was in summer physics. He wasn't there to get extra enrichment. He was there to make up credits. Was he still using drugs? And if he was, what would I do about it? Because, even if I'd learned the signs in health class, how likely was I to do what the text books said, "Go tell a teacher or counselor." I wanted to laugh out loud. I wouldn't tell a teacher or counselor if I thought Christopher was using. I didn't even know where the Counselor's office was at Cascadia, and I couldn't imagine telling Mrs. McCallister.

I doubted I'd really be able to tell if he was using drugs. His baseball coach and teammates didn't know until he tested positive. How would I know? I wouldn't. The thought made me feel better, because if I couldn't tell if he was using then I wouldn't have to worry about telling someone.

But there was another little worry plaguing me. It gnawed at the back of my mind.

No. I pushed the thought away.

It wouldn't be like Mom. It wouldn't be like it was when I wondered over and over if there was a sign. Something I missed. Something I could have done. I took a deep breath.

Thinking about all of this was exhausting.

Mrs. McCallister cleared her throat, and I looked over at her. She stared hard at her computer screen and took another swig of her coffee. Her eyebrows raised before she leaned over and began typing furiously.

I let my breath out slowly and turned back to the screen in

front of me. I was supposed to be doing a research assignment. At least that's what I told Mrs. McCallister when I arrived thirty minutes early and sat down at an empty black lab table near the front of the class. I'd pulled out my laptop and explained that the Internet connection at home had been down, and so I hoped to get some work done here. The truth was we didn't pay the cable bill which included the Internet and phone. This morning, they'd all been turned off. I hadn't gotten anything done last night on either physics or the AP literature class, not to mention the online SAT Class. I thought arriving early and looking like I wanted to get some extra work done would be in my favor— especially after the first lab disaster.

But Mrs. McCallister hadn't even gotten to the classroom yet. She hustled in ten minutes later. At first, I was pretty sure I saw a dark shadow cross her face when she saw me, which I thought was strange, because why wouldn't she be glad to see me? But, then the darkness passed, she unlocked the door, quickly turned on all the classroom lights and yanked open the blinds.

"I'm so happy to see you," she gushed before she picked up a large coffee mug and her purse. It seemed to me her purse was awful heavy and her left shoulder drooped with the weight. She left before I could really look too closely, and when she came back, she seemed much more cheerful. And, what did I care? I had a lot more to worry about than Mrs. McCallister's morning moods.

It really had been my intention to do some research on the math equations and see if I could find some models and diagrams for how to do them without having to admit to Mrs. McCallister I hadn't taken calculus yet.

But as soon as I connected to the school internet, I couldn't help myself. I Googled Christopher Parks. I wanted to know if the rumors were true. I heard Jarrod talking to another boy about how they hoped Christopher would be coming back to the baseball team, and they were sorry about what happened in the spring. I didn't want to ask Jarrod, and it seemed like everyone already knew since they all went to Cascadia. I told myself I just wanted to find out what position Christopher played, so I could talk to him about baseball.

Of course, that's not what happened, and instead of finding one or two articles about his baseball performance, I found three pages about Christopher Parks.

They were all about his drug use and being removed from the baseball team. Apparently, there had even been talk about whether the findings could be upheld in a court of law, and Christopher's civil rights may have been violated. But, that had quickly been defeated when Christopher's mom stated she was glad the truth was out in the open. Not to mention the fact all parents signed release forms giving permission for the athlete to be tested periodically for substance use.

"What'cha reading?"

Dazed, I looked up to see Christopher peering over my shoulder. His face paled, and his eyes darkened. "I see," he said.

"It's…." I stopped. We both could see what I was reading. There was no point in me trying to explain anything.

"Don't believe everything you read," Christopher dropped a thick lab packet on the table in front of me.

Silently, I closed the laptop and slipped it back into my bag. What could I say? I was snooping about him. And not something cheerful and happy like an article about how he scored the winning run in a ball game. I picked up the lab paper. "We're testing—" I said shakily.

"—Newton's laws," Christopher said. "We're going outside to run."

I turned to look out the window. What kind of crazy lab did Mrs. McCallister have for us today? It surely couldn't be as bad as the first one. If we were running, that had to mean we were on the ground. I wouldn't throw up on the ground. But, then why did my stomach feel like it wanted to upchuck? I bit down hard on my lip. Concentrate. Concentrate.

I squinted and looked toward the parking lot where I could see a tall white speedometer. It was the kind the police set out in neighborhoods that told you what speed you were going.

Mom used to like to go a little faster than the speed limit. More than once, we'd buzz past the speedometers and she'd hit the brakes. She'd glance in the rear view mirror, and then once we'd gone a couple blocks, turn and smile at me. "Guess I was lucky this time," she'd say. I wished Mom had remembered that luck a little more.

By the time I turned away from the window, Christopher was already at the classroom door. His back was to me, and he was walking with another girl. I felt like crying. I wished I could just take back the last ten minutes. Instead of reading the news articles, I should have been reading something about math, or even working on that literature paper. Christopher would have grinned at me in that slow, lazy way and none of this would have happened.

But now, when everyone else was walking with their partner and talking, I was left wondering if I was even going to be his lab partner. Wondering if what happened in my bedroom the night before was only a fluke. The girl walking with Christopher had a tattoo just above the waistband of her shorts. Her crop shirt bared her midriff. Marissa. I remembered hearing her name was Marissa. She'd been up on the roof with me yesterday. At first, I thought she might want to be partners with me. There weren't that many girls in the class, and she didn't have a partner either. But, then, when we'd gotten to the roof, she'd leaned over and yelled for Jarrod to be her partner. He'd looked up at her with a silly grin on his face and agreed.

I walked slowly behind them, and debated about what to do. I could ignore Christopher and hope someone else would be my partner. If Marissa was Christopher's partner, then Jarrod wouldn't have one. I quickly scanned the cluster of kids by the speedometer. I couldn't tell which one he was, everyone blended together.

I thought about turning around and telling Mrs. McCallister I didn't feel well. I could ask for a make-up and a pass to the Nurse. Of course, I didn't know if Cascadia had a nurse in the summer, and maybe she'd just send me back home, and that didn't sound appealing either because then I'd have to explain to Dad why I was home early.

Or, I could walk up to Marissa and Christopher. I could pretend everything was fine. I liked that option the best. Wasn't that what I'd always done when there was trouble? I just pretended everything would work out. And it usually did.

Suddenly, Marissa stopped and dropped back to me. "He's moody sometimes."

"What?" It was hard not to stare at Marissa. Her shirt came half way to her cropped pants and everything was so tight I could see her ribs. Marissa snapped her spearmint gum. Her sharp dark eyes roamed up and down me as if she was inspecting something she wasn't sure if she wanted to buy or not.

Marissa rolled her eyes and pointed her thumb at Christopher's back. "Moody."

"I think he's mad at me." I didn't think it was fair for Melissa to talk about him behind his back. I wanted her to know there was a reason for Christopher's mood.

"He'll get it over it." Marissa tossed back her head and let out a peal of laughter. "Watch."

But before I could watch anything, Mrs. McCallister's sharp whistle and the thud of shoes hitting the pavement made me swing around. Half the class was running, and it was easy to see Christopher was ahead of everyone else. I had to hurry to the finish line to get his score. As soon as Christopher crossed the line, I'd walk over and talk to him, tell him I was sorry. Explain I only wanted to find out what position he played on the baseball team. My hands shook as I smoothed my lab paper and uncapped my pen.

Mrs. McCallister blew her whistle as Christopher flashed by. I looked at the speedometer and then, carefully, I wrote down Christopher's time.

I could do this. I could figure out the math problem. The numbers swirled in front of me, as tears formed in the corners of my eyes.

I couldn't do it. The math was over my head.

And, when I looked up, Christopher was talking to Marissa.

Their heads were pressed together as she leaned in close to him. Marissa placed her hand on his arm, threw back her head, and let out another shriek of laughter.

"Shantel," Ms. McCallister said abruptly. "Are you finished with the lab? It doesn't take that long to record times, and do the simple equation."

Mutely, I held out my assignments to her. The paper shook in the wind, and I didn't make any move to steady it.

Ms. McCallister glanced at the empty equations and snapped, "The lab is only partially finished. This is not what I expect from you."

I yanked the paper back to my chest and held it close to me. I wasn't going to let Marissa monopolize Christopher's attention. I straightened my shoulders, and with my head held high, walked over to them.

Marissa turned slyly to me, and with a catlike smile that sent panic streaking through my chest, placed her fingers over Christopher's lips. Her pink painted tips moved slowly over his mouth.

Never in a million years would I have the nerve to run my fingertips over Christopher's lips. But Christopher seemed to have gone into some kind of trance. He gazed at her like she was the only one in the crowded parking lot before she removed her fingers and said, "Later."

Then, she glided off in a sultry walk across the parking lot.

The lab packet slipped from my hands and I didn't try to catch it.

CHAPTER TEN

Christopher

I paced outside the science wing. Why did Shantel have to find those articles? I wanted to be the one to tell her; in my own time, in my own way. Explain how I was going to Meetings, staying sober. She could even come with me to a Meeting, if she wanted. But now, she'd seen all that stuff in the papers. And more was coming. The reporters finally got ahold of Mom and convinced her to let them do an article; not just on Dad's arrest, but our whole family. They called it a feature story and we were the feature. They wanted to focus on my sobriety, and said it would inspire others to overcome challenges. I didn't like it, and I don't know why she would agree to something like that, I certainly didn't want anything to do with it.

Panic made my chest hurt and it was hard to breathe. I couldn't just stand by and watch everything slip out of my control. I waited in the empty courtyard, hoping she would appear at any minute, and I could tell her, well, I wasn't sure what, but I had to see her. I turned so I could see the Science Wing where Shantel disappeared ten minutes ago.

A group of girls strolled past with Marissa at the lead. "Hey, Christopher," Marissa said. "We're all going to get something to eat, wanna come?"

"Waiting on someone," I said.

Marissa shook her head. "Don't do anything I wouldn't."

Marissa swung her hips and sashayed in an exaggerated walk. She turned around, and winked at me. I smiled. It was an old game. Both Marissa and I were well aware of who she belonged to—Michael. I had listened to Marissa's drunken tears, regularly driven her home from parties after Michael left to make a quick deal, and even taken her to get a tattoo. While I was in treatment, Marissa came to visit a couple times. But, after briefly listening to me talk about my treatment and how things were going, Marissa launched into the latest drama about Michael. I knew nothing would pry her away from him and I didn't really want it to, either. Melissa had too much drama for me.

Frowning, I stared at the science wing. Where is she? I thought about going to go find out when I heard, "Waiting on someone?"

Michael jostled my arm. "You just missed Marissa."

Michael shrugged. "I'll catch her later." He reached into his pocket and pulled out a large tablet. "On me."

I took a good look around the courtyard for the usual on-campus officer who strolled up and down after summer classes. It used to be a real police officer until the school lost some of its funding. Now the "officer" was only a parent volunteer, which was a good thing for Michael and his business. Parent volunteers weren't always real sure what they were seeing. Especially when it was Michael, whose dad is a judge who's donated a lot of money to the school fundraisers.

"Not now," I managed to mutter. Inside, I was shaking. Just the sight of that one magic bullet sent my heart racing. All this worry about Shantel would disappear if I took just one tablet. I could just place that pill on my tongue, and let it dissolve. In minutes, there would be a nice little buzz, and I would be thinking I could do anything.

"Trying to help." Michael pocketed the temptation. "'Cause I know you need a little something right now. You look like you're about to puke." He snorted.

"I'm fine."

"Yeah? Well, if you're not..." He stepped up so close I can feel his breath in my face, "You know where to find me."

"Yeah," I said. "I know."

This time it wasn't like when he was trying to set me up. This time, Michael was just doing what we've always done when I liked some girl. His job was to provide me with a little something. A little something that would help take the edge off, and make me feel like I was King of the World. Once I swallowed that medicine, all the awful worries would vanish, and I would be in control again. At least that was what I thought, but part of me knew it wasn't true.

I wiped the sweat off my forehead. It wasn't so easy staying sober one day at a time. My tongue felt thick and dry against the roof of my mouth. I fumbled in my bag for a water bottle. I sifted through my English book and notebooks, but came up with nothing. It was the perfect excuse to go into the science room. I would say I was just looking for my water bottle. No one would realize I was checking for Shantel. I picked up my bag and headed across the empty campus, marveling at how fast everything cleared out in the summer. There were no clubs or sports practices and no one wanted to be at school for a second longer than necessary.

I entered the science wing and stepped inside the hallway. The concrete walls were stripped of their colorful posters announcing upcoming sporting events or student elections. The classroom doors were all shut. Except for a small light shining from under the door of the physics room, the hall was like a ghost town.

I walked down the hall and pulled open the physics door. I stopped in my tracks and stared in disbelief. McCallister was sitting on a small stool in the corner of the room and taking a long drink of something that was definitely not water. I froze. My feet wouldn't move and any words I could think of were trapped inside my throat.

"Do you need something?" McCallister slipped the small bottle under her desk without flinching.

"Water bottle," I mumbled, released from my inertia by the sound of her voice. I dashed to the front lab table, located and grabbed my water bottle. I held it up to show her. I felt as if I was the one doing something wrong. I shifted on the balls of my feet like I used to when I got in trouble for talking too much in middle school. I didn't have a clue what to say to her and I sure didn't want to stick around until she said something to me. I put my head down and scurried out of the room. If I had a sweatshirt, the hood would be over my head. I wished I could make myself invisible.

It's not my business if McCallister wants a drink or two after class. But, drinking in her classroom, by herself, was not just an occasional drink. Nope, McCallister seemed to have a little problem—just like me. Charlie would tell me to help her. He'd say it was a great opportunity to share the Twelve Steps. But, I wasn't about to try and Twelve Step her into the Meetings.

I hustled outside and scanned the bus stop for Shantel. No sign of her. I knew just where to go.

I hopped in the truck, and turned toward Shantel's farm.

Fifteen minutes later, I was coasting into her driveway. I had an excuse to be there—it wasn't just about making up for what happened in physics. The broken loom part was inside my glove compartment. It was a genius idea to tell her I'd fix it. I always liked to fix things, and this was pretty easy. A little trip to the hardware store, a few nails, a bit of hammering, and the part was as good as new.

I parked my truck by the house and took my time getting out. My heart pounded like crazy. I never noticed how hard it was or how much energy it took to be around girls. Of course, I always used to have a little something to help me out with these feelings, and now I felt like I was stripped bare.

I stepped up to Shantel's front door, moving the small piece of wood back and forth in my hands. The nervous butterflies danced around in my stomach. When I was using, I never had time to feel the butterflies. I covered nerves up with a quick fix. Now, it seemed like everything I did made me nervous. Calm down, Parks, I tell myself like it's a big game. Everything is under control.

"Hello?" I called through the screen door. Someone had to be home. The front door was open to the screen. I leaned over and grabbed a couple colorful flowers from a silver pitcher on a small wood table next to the door. Girls always love flowers.

The sloping green hillside reminded me of when I was a child and made a slippery slide on hot summer days. Dad showed me how to take one of the blue tarps, which usually covered the wood pile, and spread it out in the yard. We poured Mom's dish soap into a plastic bucket with water. Dad stood on the edge of the plastic sheet while I jumped and slid on the tarp.

I stared down the hillside and saw long legs draped over a white hammock. The hammock swung back and forth in the wind. I knew who was on that hammock. I tucked the piece of wood into my pocket and jogged down the hill. The wind blew in my face, and cooled off the small bead of sweat rolling down the side of my face. I hoped my shirt wasn't getting all pitted out. That could be embarrassing.

I pulled myself to a halt before I came up on the hammock. I checked my underarms. Everything looked dry and normal. No bands of sweat. Everything dry. The hammock rocked gently, Shantel wasn't aware of my presence yet. She leaned over and picked up a strawberry from a bowl. She popped the strawberry into her mouth without pausing in her reading. My mouth watered. I wanted one of those strawberries. It seemed like I was always hungry since I'd been sober.

"Can I have one?"

"What?" Shantel jumped and the hammock swung wildly.

"Hold on there," I said as I grabbed the hammock. I tried hard to ignore the red strawberry juice around her mouth. All I could think of was licking it off.

"What are you doing?"

I wanted to reassure her I wasn't stalking her. I just wanted to give her the loom part.

"I brought you something." Nervously, I held out the crumpled flowers in my right hand, and with my left hand pulled the mended piece of the loom from my pocket.

Shantel gawked at me like I'd lost my mind. I was beginning to think maybe I might have. I wanted to tell her I was sorry about my response to the news article. But I couldn't make the words form in my mouth.

It takes a lot of courage to admit I've done something wrong. In the Meetings the Old Timers say it's part of staying sober—you gotta admit when you do something wrong. But nobody talked about how hard it was to say those words. My gut churned.

"Okay." Shantel took the wood from my hand. Her eyes pulled me in, deep and fathomless.

I could drown in those eyes.

CHAPTER ELEVEN

Shantel

I tossed my romance novel to the ground and made sure the cover was down. After the disaster with physics, I'd gone to Advanced Literature and explained I wasn't feeling well. It was the truth. I wasn't feeling good. Mrs. Smoot looked at me like she knew I was lying, but she gave me the assignment and told me to rest. She reminded me summer classes were intense, and since I already missed two days, it was beginning to be doubtful if I would be able to earn credit for the session. I didn't want to think about Dad's disappointment in me.

I caught the bus to the bakery, and then gave Mia the same story about why I couldn't work in the bakery. Mia hadn't been too happy, and with Owen screaming in the background, she called Jeff and told him I needed a ride to the farm, because I wasn't feeling well. They had a few heated words before Mia hung up, whirled around to face me, and said, "I hope this isn't a pattern."

By the time, Jeff dropped me off, I did feel sick. Very sick. Sick with the amount of lying I'd been doing. The internet and phone still was off, so I took my romance novel and went to the hammock. If Mom was here, she would have understood, I thought darkly. She would have let me curl into the bed, with a cold washcloth, and shut curtains, just like she used to.

I carefully set the loom piece on the other side of the book. My heart was pounding. How long had he been standing there? Watching me? I'd been so lost in my story I hadn't heard his truck, or him. Christopher was the last person I expected to see.

"Nice place." Christopher waved his hands at the surrounding hillside. "It reminds me of a circus camp."

"Circus camp?"

"I wanted to be a performer in the circus. For about three years, I went to this camp where all we did was learn about circus performances."

His face shone with happiness, and his blue eyes sparkled. I realized there was a lot I didn't know about Christopher. "Do you still go?"

"No," Christopher shook his head, and a shadow passed over his face. "Got involved with some other things."

I didn't say anything. I knew what those other things were.

"But, I'm sober now." Christopher looked me directly in the eye.

"That's good," I said brightly. I didn't know what else to say. Once again, the health class books hadn't exactly written out a conversation you might have with someone who had used drugs but didn't anymore.

"Yes," Christopher leaned forward. Our faces were so close I could smell his minty breath. And without hesitating, I lifted my face to him. Very softly, he touched his lips to mine. I sighed as he pulled me closer. His lips moved softly against my mouth. His hands wandered up and through my hair, and he gently pried open my lips with his. I shifted and positioned myself so I leaned into him. The hammock swayed under us.

"It's hot," Christopher murmured against my lips. He leaned away from me and pulled his shirt out of his pants.

I moved over in the hammock and Christopher lay down beside me. His arms wrapped around me and he pulled me so we lay side-by-side. I wound my legs through his, our bare skin pressed together.

"Nice," Christopher whispered against my cheek and rubbed circles on my back. Christopher's hands didn't stay on my back for long. Instead, they crept lower until he hovered above my waist line. I was nervous. But, I didn't want him to stop. This time I was not going to pull away, I was going to be more like Marissa, and act like I knew just what to do.

His hand crept lower, and, with a quick flick of his fingers, moved inside my shorts. I tried to breathe and pretend what was happening was something I expected and knew how to handle. Christopher's finger trailed a light touch up my thigh before stopping and resting on top of my cotton underwear. He raised himself up on his arm and waited. "Okay?"

"Okay," I whispered. It felt like I'd been waiting forever.

The hammock swung gently with our movement and I closed my eyes while Christopher let his fingers explore.

When it was over, Christopher straightened my clothes before gathering me in a soft embrace. I rolled up on my elbow and studied him. I knew we hadn't done all that much. At least not in comparison to what I'd heard from other people. But I wondered, would he think less of me now? Would I think less of me? The sweat glistened on his forehead, and his eyes were closed. Suddenly, I realized Christopher had his own needs and something in what just happened made him want something too. I was unsure what to do, but I moved so we weren't so close.

"It's okay." Christopher breathed deeply beside me. He opened his eyes and looked into mine. "It's okay."

He rolled slightly away from me, and lazily dropped his hand to the ground. Slowly, he brought up my paperback book. "What's this?" He turned it over to see the cover.

"Don't," I cried and tried to yank the book away from him.

"Why not?" Christopher continued to hold the book out of reach. "This looks kinda interesting." In a stage voice, and with a straight face, Christopher began to read. "He opened up the door to find her lying across the bed in a red bra."

"It doesn't say that," I protested and then giggled. He sounded so funny and looked so serious. It was as if he was reading from a science text book.

"No?" Christopher grinned and then dropped the book to the ground. "Then what does it say?"

"I don't know," I said as the color flooded my face. I couldn't believe we were talking about my romance book.

"Mmm…" Christopher flipped through another couple of pages before I yanked it out of his hand.

"I think it says he swept her off her feet, and…."

In one giant swoop, Christopher yanked hard on the hammock, and sent me tumbling to the ground.

"…she falls hard for him." Christopher leaned down and kissed me again.

CHAPTER TWELVE

Christopher

On Saturday mornings, I always met with Charlie. It is a one-on-one where I am supposed to work on the Twelve Steps. We go to the diner which is a street over from the bakery. Today, I was a little early and took a detour to drive by the bakery. I was pretty sure Shantel said she helped out on Saturday. And sure enough, when I cruised by slowly, she was wiping a table near the front. Wearing an apron, and with her hair tied back in a ponytail, she looked a lot different than she did in physics, or on the hammock. Suddenly, her head jerked up and she looked out the window.

Guilt surged through me, like I just got caught doing something I shouldn't. Without thinking I gunned the truck without waving. It was a dumb thing to do, but I had felt out of sorts for the last two days. I wasn't sure what was wrong with me. I was all fired up when I left Shantel. I even got a kick out of the whole romance book thing, but then, something took over. Probably my addict brain. It started telling me I was worthless, I would never be a romance hero, and she was wasting her time with me. My addict mind started telling me I ought to give it all up now, give it up before I got hurt.

If I wasn't careful, I would start acting on those feelings, and I didn't want to. I hoped the meeting with Charlie would help me get back on track again. I needed to get it straight before physics on Monday.

I found a parking spot, got out and opened the diner door. I smelled bacon, eggs and brewing coffee. Lots of coffee. The diner had green plastic seats and small tables. Most of the tables were full. I nodded to Dan, Bill, and Greg, clustered at a table by the window. Half the time, I thought the coffee shop was just an extension of the church basement. Every time Charlie and I met, there were always AA guys in here. They sucked down coffee and discussed their life Step stories.

"Coffee?" Charlie asked as I eased into the booth. It's the kind of seat where my legs stuck to the plastic when it was hot. Angie, the waitress, held the steaming pot toward the small white coffee cups. She smiled and the lines around her eyes and mouth crinkled. She served us the first time I met with Charlie. That time, I was so nervous I ended up spilling my coffee. Angie didn't say a word, just rushed over and wiped everything down. She patted me on the shoulder and told me everything was going to be fine. Angie must have been used to a lot of spilled coffee and nervous guys meeting with their sponsors the first time.

"No coffee." I covered my empty white cup with my right hand. "A soda?" I still hadn't gotten used to having coffee every time I went to Meetings. The Steps and Meetings are supposed to lead me to a better life. A life filled with integrity and honesty. But it always seemed to involve a lot of coffee.

"Sure, love," Angie said as she picked up my empty glass, and walked away from us. Her thick soled, white shoes squished on the linoleum floor.

I shifted uneasily and fiddled with my fork. Charlie tapped my hand. "It's okay. Everyone is nervous about the Fourth Step."

Slowly, I dropped the fork back to the paper napkin. By now, I should trust Charlie. We've worked the first three steps. I've learned about being powerless over my addiction. That part didn't seem too hard to get. It was pretty obvious when I landed in treatment for a dirty UA I was powerless over something. But, Charlie said that's not all the Step means. The Step was about understanding that I was powerless over my addict, too. That addict voice was the same voice telling me I wasn't so good for Shantel. And right now, I didn't feel so powerless over that voice. We've also worked the steps that say my life has become insane and a Higher Power can restore me to sanity. I didn't really believe too much in a Higher Power. We never went to Church all that much, only on holidays like Christmas and Easter, and we haven't gone once since Dad went to prison. Charlie says my Higher Power can be anything—even the door knob. I thought that was kinda funny.

But we weren't talking about being powerless or Higher Powers today. Today we were taking an inventory. I had heard all about the Fourth Step in Meetings. It was the one they called the killer Step. I was supposed to make an inventory, or a list, of all my faults. I hoped I don't have that many. I was only sixteen. How many faults could I really have?

Charlie handed me a blank napkin and a pen. "Ready?"

"Sure," I said. What other choice was there at that point?

We spent the next hour making a four column list. I listed the people, places, and things I felt resentment about. Charlie said it was okay to write things on there like traffic lights and speed signs. I had a lot of resentments about those. The cops liked to pull me over, and I had a bunch of tickets Charlie said I would have to get straightened out soon.

After I finished, Charlie asked me to list what my part was in the situation. Sometimes it was easy to see. Like the time my guidance counselor wanted me to take anger management classes after I'd been in three fights at school.

Or the time Michael and I went skinny dipping in the hotel pool after the Championship baseball game. We were higher than kites, and had a great time splashing around. But the next day, the coaches and the hotel management gave the whole team a lecture about being positive role models. Skinny dipping, in a hotel pool, was not considered good sportsmanship. By that time, the high had worn off anyway and I couldn't figure out what we had been thinking.

Other times it was a little murky, like with Marissa. I could see how, sometimes, the things we said or did with each other might cause someone else harm. I thought of Shantel and how she looked when Marissa ran her finger across my lip. Marissa was always touching me, and we both knew it didn't really mean anything. It's just the way Marissa was and how she liked to get attention.

Charlie nudged me to think about my family too. He said most of the harm comes to family members. I knew he was right. I wasn't proud of how I used to show up stoned to events like Thanksgiving or Christmas Eve dinner. Mom would have gone all out to make everything nice, used the good silver and china. Then I'd show up, half-stoned out of my mind. I'd argue with everyone, ruin the meal, make Mom cry.... I added Mom's name to the list.

Charlie encouraged me, telling me I was doing great. By this time, I was pretty tired, and my soda was drained to the last ice cube. All the other guys had left, and I could tell by my watch we had been sitting in the booth for a long time.

"What about your dad?" Charlie prodded. He eyed me with a gaze that made me want to sink to the ground.

"Dad," I repeated. Suddenly, the adrenaline pumped through me like I was about to hit a ball out of the park for a winning run.

"How do you feel about him?" "Why?"

Charlie stared at me, and I looked away. We both knew he was asking how I felt about Dad being arrested. And that was a question which wasn't so easy to answer, because there were a whole lot of feelings about Dad. Feelings I didn't have names for; feelings that made me ball up inside and feel like I was tied in a hundred different little knots; feelings that came hard and fast and made me want to run to the opposite ends of the universe to escape them.

The other night, Dad called. The phone had a strange buzz on the other end, and then a computerized voice said, "Call from Prisoner 6724, will you accept?" Once I said yes, Dad was there. "Hey, Chris," he said. "How you holding up?" As if I was the one in jail, and he was at home. The conversation didn't last long before we were interrupted and cut off. I was left holding the empty line.

"Fine," I told Charlie. "I feel fine."

"Really?" Charlie pressed me harder for a real answer. "Your Dad was arrested. And you feel fine?"

"Sure," I shrugged like it was no big deal and pushed my Fourth Step paper toward him.

Charlie ignored the paper.

"I gotta get going." I dropped a couple dollars beside my list on the table. My heart was beating a million miles a minute. This AA stuff was supposed to be about me staying clean and sober, one day at a time. It was not supposed to be about Dad. It was not supposed to be about me and Dad. What did Dad have to do with keeping me sober?

I backed out of the parking lot and decided to take the long way home. I needed time to think. Well, that's what I told myself. I just needed some time to think. But, of course, my long way home took me past the hillside with the two-story Craftsman houses, and the house where we lived before we moved into the big house in the new subdivision. The hill was in the older section of town and had a sweeping view of the valley and river below. I always loved our house. The hardwood floors had just a slight tilt to them and the front yards often had a few extra cars parked on the lawn because there were no driveways. Mom sometimes complained we lived in a junk yard with all the extra cars up on blocks, and people fixing them on weekends. But I liked the sound of the whirling drills and voices which carried through our open windows.

The house still looked the same, and the blueberry bushes that Dad planted have berries on them. Dad didn't belong on my resentment list, did he? My head hurt, and something inside was dragging me down. Deep far down to a place I didn't want to go.

I cruised slowly down the street and then turned left and toward Willow Ridge. We moved to Willow Ridge when Mom got her real estate license. She said she got a good deal on the sale of the house because she was one of the real estate agents helping out with the sale of the development. I liked Willow Ridge for other reasons. While the houses were under construction, Michael and I had a playground of partially-built homes. Once the houses were framed, they offered more than enough corners on a summer night for other pursuits. Of course, we weren't studying architecture inside those houses. We were studying how to get high, and, sometimes, finding out how far a girl might go when tucked away inside the skeleton rooms where no one could interrupt us.

I turned into our driveway and very carefully parked my truck along the left side. In the summer, the sky stayed light until almost ten-o-clock. Evening was a good time to run, and maybe, a quick jog would help me get rid of the awful feeling inside right now.

I opened the screen door and dropped my keys in the basket. The large screen TV was on full blast. I knew if Mom were home she'd have something to say. The first time Alex and I sat down to watch a movie we'd turned the sound up high, because how else did you watch the latest James Bond movie? We settled in with a big bowl of buttery popcorn. And then Mom stormed into the family room. She yelled about the noise of the TV and scooped up the bright yellow bowl of popcorn right out of our laps. She placed the bowl on the kitchen table and instructed us to eat at the table and not on the new leather couches. We tried to tell her the point was to eat popcorn in front of the TV, not off to the side. But she didn't get it. Now, the only time we cranked the TV up high was when Mom wasn't home.

"Alex," I hollered over the noise.

Alex was sitting on the floor, staring halfheartedly at the screen. Papers and a grade school history book lay on the floor around him. Mom didn't believe in idle summers. As soon as she found out the school was offering special enrichment summer classes for elementary school, she signed Alex up. Between classes and soccer camp, the poor kid seemed to have no free time. I felt bad for him.

Alex muttered something incoherent. I stepped around the couch and grabbed the remote. I turned down the volume and got a look at Alex's face. A large, deep purple bruise spread across his check. I whistled.

"What happened to you?"

"I got in a fight." Alex wouldn't look at me and continued to stare at the TV.

"I can see that. Ice will help." I went into the kitchen and yanked the freezer open. I knew we had frozen veggies. We always had frozen veggies. Mom kept them just in case. No one mentioned my fighting days. The most painful part was right after the fight, when the eye was swollen and puffy.

Alex trailed after me and leaned against the kitchen counter. "It wasn't my fault."

"Yea?" I handed over the package of frozen peas. "Was it Dad?"

Alex didn't say anything, but he winced. I hit the truth.

"Does Mom know?"

"They called her." Alex shrugged. He stared at the package like he'd never seen peas before. "It's a fight. I got a couple days suspension from summer camp."

"Hold this up there," I nodded toward his eye. "Swelling will go down."

Alex flinched as he put the frozen peas against his eye.

"Come on." I motioned toward the door. "I want to show you something."

"What?" Alex eyed me warily through his one good eye.

I winked at him. "Magic."

CHAPTER THIRTEEN

Shantel

I stared out the large front window of the bakery. Christopher's blue truck disappeared from view. Even though I knew it was pointless, I placed my hands on the round glass table and leaned forward to look out the window.

My heart pounded with unanswered questions. Why didn't he stop? He saw me. Our eyes met. I looked up from wiping the table, and in that brief moment, our eyes had met. But he didn't stop, and he didn't wave. Was it because of what happened in the hammock? I thought everything was fine when Christopher left. Did something happen to change his mind? It had been two days, and I hadn't really heard from him. I knew not to text him. I didn't want to look like I was desperate. I'd heard the boys talking about the girls who chased them. They didn't like it. So, I'd been trying not to think about it. Maybe he didn't have my number, or maybe something was wrong with his phone, or maybe someone happened, someone like Marissa. I bit down hard on my lip, looked down, and saw the headlines of the paper:

WILLIAM PARKS AWAITING SENTENCING:
PRISON IS NOT JUST FOR THE PRISONER.

The picture showed Christopher with his fists clenched. His posture was rigid, as were the muscles in his jaw. He stood by the side of his brother, Alex. Christopher's mom stood behind them. Her face was pale and drawn. Her hands rested on the boys' shoulders—as if they were holding her upright. I kept reading.

Prison is not just for the prisoner. Instead of spending Saturdays at the park or ball field, Christopher Parks, and younger brother Alex, will spend their Saturdays visiting their father, William Parks, at the Monroe State Penitentiary. Parks is currently awaiting trial in what looks to be a guilty plea for embezzlement of State funds from the auditing office. When asked how the boys feel about visiting their father, Christopher shrugged and said, "No comment."

Sometimes, organizations such as The Volunteers of America or Matthew House provide activities for families, including art and poetry. But, when asked if the boys will continue to visit their Dad once he is sentenced, Allison Parks only shook her head. "We can't think that far ahead. It's really been a struggle. I'm a single parent who is working and going back to school to earn a degree in commercial real-estate. It's not easy," Allison said. "But we make it work. Christopher is a great help to me, and I'm so proud of him."

"Shantel." Mia tapped me on the shoulder.

Her lavender lotion perfume floated around me in a misty haze.

"Sorry," I mumbled and tossed the paper upside down. "I'll finish this up."

"Is everything okay?" Mia peered into my eyes, and I looked away.

"Sure." I wiped hard at a nonexistent spot on the table. I was not going to tell Mia I saw Christopher and he didn't stop or wave—even though he had seen me. She'd probably seen the article. Everyone read the small town paper. I didn't want to talk about it.

Mia continued to watch me. "You were so quiet last night and now this morning, well..." she paused. "I don't know. I thought maybe you might want to talk about it."

"I'm fine." I picked up a red mosaic globe candle holder and placed it in the small cardboard box with the others. Talking about things led you nowhere.

Dad took me to a psychologist once. He wanted me to talk about how I felt about Mom. I spent the whole hour talking about how death could be looked at in terms of biology, and the human body. Fifty minutes later, the psychologist rubbed her eyes, and told Dad maybe there was someone else who would be a better choice for me.

Dad hadn't pursued finding someone else and that was the end of me talking to anyone.

I slipped the last of the globe candles into the box, and headed toward the small closet to the left of the bakery door. Last night, the romance book group gathered around tables pushed together in the center of the bakery. Before they arrived, I'd pulled out the box of globe candles, which Mia kept for special occasions, and set one on every table. Mia served her special chocolates tortes, and we spent hours talking about Love's Last Whisper. Well, everyone else spent hours talking, and I spent hours listening.

I wanted a play book I could use for the next time Christopher and I were together. I wanted instructions like the kind that came with lab work. I figured the best place to find instructions to love would be the romance book club. I paid special attention when the conversations turned to the romantic scenes in the book. Maybe someone would veer off the book and start talking about their lives. I was particularly glad for the darkened bakery. I didn't want anyone to know I was trying to study a romance novel as if I was preparing for a big test.

I finished wiping the tables and threaded my way through the line of customers toward the back of the bakery. The bakery was busy this morning, and it was almost one o'clock before I looked up at the clock again.

Mia wiped the sweat off her forehead. "Do you want soup?"

I shook my head. "I better go. I have some homework to do." The truth was I'd finished all my homework. I'd caught up on all my reading in the literature class, completed the physics pre-lab work for Monday, and even managed to work in three assignments of the SAT prep class.

"Can you take that to Gloria?" Mia asked. "I forgot to give it to her last night."

I grabbed the paperback novel from the counter. It was the second in a historical fiction series we read two months ago. I didn't think it was very good. The heroine was captured on a pirate ship, and it seemed to me she could have gotten free about half-way through the book. I untied my apron, and placed it on the counter. I picked up the book, and headed for the back screen door of the bakery. Once outside, I turned down the back alley toward the Children's Theater. I could easily slip in the back door, and lay the book on Gloria's desk.

When I opened up the door, Gloria's office door was closed, and I could hear voices coming from the theater. Curious, I made my way toward the theater and slipped into the back left corner.

On the stage, Christopher leaned down to a boy who looked about eight-years-old. Christopher patiently showed the boy how to hook and unhook metal rings. When the boy couldn't unhook the rings, Christopher gently took the rings from the boy. He showed him, again, how to unhook the rings.

In the dark theater, I sank into a chair in the back and set the book on the floor. All time stopped as I kicked off my shoes and tucked my legs up underneath me on the old, cracked and peeling leather theater seat.

Christopher was a marvel to watch. He moved effortlessly through card tricks, ring tricks, and a rabbit hat trick. I forgot about not liking magic, and became entranced with how each trick unfolded. Each time he finished, Christopher repeated the trick for the boy. He'd be a good instructor at Gloria's summer theater camps.

I'd never been brave enough to take any of Gloria's summer camps, which of course, contradicted Mom who had always called me the baby that sizzled. "Baby, you're going to set the world on fire," she'd say to me as she combed my hair at night. Mom thought sizzling started with my birthday. She said I had the best birthday in the world—July 21. Mom said Leo cusp was a good sign, enough fire to be a leader, and enough Cancer to know how to follow. Mom took me to an astrologer once, who told her I'd always be a backstage girl. Mom yanked me out of the astrologer's office.

"Don't listen to her," She'd said. "You're going to be a shining star. A sizzling, shining star."

For a long time, I tried to be Mom's sizzling, shining star. But in elementary school, I threw up before every oral report. In middle school drama, I chose to be a tree where I could hide behind tall leafy branches and a thick trunk. But Mom did not give up. She took me to a therapist who tried to pry into the depths of my mind. She took me to a hypnotist who attempted to find out which of my past lives had been so traumatic. She even tried to feed me herbal remedies. Nothing worked. Eventually Mom gave up. "I think you are more a scientist like your Dad," she'd said in frustration.

I didn't know how long I sat and watched Christopher, but when Gloria's voice echoed through the theater I pretty much about fell out of my seat.

"Shantel! I didn't know you were here! What are you doing in the dark?"

"I brought your book," I mumbled. I scooped the paperback off the floor. Meekly, I held it out to her. I didn't dare look at the stage. There was no way Christopher didn't hear Gloria. Her voice was well-practiced for the theater and whether she was on-stage or not, she was loud. I looked at my watch and sucked in my breath. I'd been watching Christopher for twenty minutes. He was going to think I was stalking him! This was far worse than if I'd called or texted him.

Gloria took the book and frowned as she looked toward the stage. Her short dark hair cropped around her thin face and accented her angular features. Gloria looked every bit the part of the harsh director and critic.

"Christopher! Birthday party tricks are not going to work on that stage. No one is going to be entertained. You need to do your father's tricks."

Gloria was a shrewd business woman. She had to be to keep the theater open. But, the edge in her voice made me gasp.

Christopher didn't miss a beat. He replied with the same sharpness in his voice, "I was waiting on my assistant back there."

I whirled around to look behind me. I half expected to see Marissa come walking out of the back.

"Good." Gloria tapped me on the shoulder. "Check the costume room for something to wear, and if not, check with Mia."

"Something to wear?" I shook my head. What was she talking about? If I came to the show I would wear a simple skirt and t-shirt.

"For the show, Shantel," Christopher said as he casually walked down the aisle toward me. "That's why you were hiding out here in the back for the past half hour, isn't it? You want to be my assistant." He gave me his lazy, sexy grin.

"Your assistant?" I muttered.

"My assistant," Christopher said as he dropped his arm over me, and pulled me close. From a distant place far away, I heard myself say, "I'll be your assistant."

CHAPTER FOURTEEN

Christopher

Shantel cuddled up against me, and for a minute, I forgot all about Alex and Gloria. Gloria cleared her throat. "Be right back," I said and gently pulled myself away from Shantel.

I moved toward the theater's supply cabinet. It was just on the other side of the stage and I doubted anyone had moved Dad's old magic props. I hummed happily. The world was at my fingertips. A genius moment when everything comes together, a Higher Power moment is what the guys in the Meetings say. The old timers say a Higher Power moment is when things come together. It's when a Higher Power does for you what you can't do for yourself. I'm pretty sure the Higher Power put Shantel right in my path so she can be my assistant. It was perfect.

When I reached the supply cabinet, I placed my hand on the door knob. My stomach churned and my vision blurred a bit, like I might throw up or something. The large closet was always off-limits to me as a child. "No one goes into that closet, but me," Dad once told me after he found me near the door.

"Why?" I had stared at the dark black door hoping it might be like the wardrobe in the Narnia story. I would open it and find a whole other world. "What happens behind the door?" I knew Dad stored his props in the closet. He folded the long, rectangular two part box used for cutting the woman in half and wheeled it to the back of the closet. Then, he placed the square box, which he used for exchanging places with his assistant, inside as well. This box appeared heavy to the audience, but it was actually lightweight. The last item was always the straight jacket. It was a real straight jacket Dad had been able to convince the local hospital to donate. He never told me what happened behind the door, and now, I was going to find out. I gave the door a hard yank like I remembered Dad doing.

"It swells shut," he'd mutter.

But someone must have stopped the swelling because the door opened easily. I took a large step backward, to steady myself, before entering the dark closet.

Memories of Dad engulfed me, almost as if I could hear him inside the closet. I found the light string above my head and yanked it. I ran my finger along one of the boxes. A thick layer of dust coated my index finger. I remembered how Dad brought the props to life with his magic. But now, he was trapped behind steel doors where no magic could ever open the doors.

I shook my head and reminded myself I had to deal with the task at hand. This was not the time to think about Dad.

I did a quick inventory. Everything seemed to be there. The woman-who-gets–cut-in-two box, the straight jacket, and the box to exchange places with the assistant. I hoped Dad's black book was tucked into one of the props. I wasn't real sure how to do all the tricks, especially the one with the swords. I needed Dad's magic book to tell me the secrets. Dad recorded all of the ways to do a trick in the black book. He made notes on tricks that worked; tricks that didn't work; diagrams, and outlines. "Just in case," he always said.

I leaned down and peered into the small crevice between the wall and the women who gets cut in two box. I ran my hand along the box and found the velvet pocket I knew was there. I slipped my hand inside. Nothing. From the stage, Alex's voice rose in what sounded like an argument. Forget the black book. I needed to get back. Fast. I didn't want something to explode between Shantel and Alex.

But I couldn't just walk out without taking anything. So,

I grabbed the heavy straightjacket. I wanted to show Shantel real magic was more than a pencil up my nose, and if she was going to be my assistant, she had to learn the tricks. I lugged the straight jacket out of the closet and hoped I could remember the knack of getting out of it. It had been over four years since Dad explained it to me. In that time, I grew from a small, under-four foot, twelve-year-old, to an almost-six foot, sixteen-year-old. The trick depended on quick maneuvers, and I hoped I didn't mess it up.

I shut the closet door, and pushed aside the stage curtain. Alex scowled at Shantel. Shantel shook her head and glared at him. I shuddered under the fierceness of her gaze. I wasn't sure what happened, but, I know how to diffuse anger. I did what I've always done—divert everyone's attention.

"Ladies and Gentleman!" My voice boomed across the empty auditorium. "You are about to see the World's Greatest Magician and..." I motioned toward Shantel with my little finger.

She raised one eyebrow at me. I grinned. "Come here."
"Why?"

I dropped the jacket onto the stage, hopped off, and in one swoop lifted her into my arms. Shantel wiggled and I clutched her tighter to me. I enjoyed every moment. It was almost like one of those romance books she reads. The hero sweeps the heroine off her feet.

"Stop! Put me down!" Her small fists beat against my chest.

"I want you on the stage, Ms. Assistant." I whispered against her left ear. I leaned down and placed a large, sloppy, very wet kiss on her cheek. She stopped beating my chest.

I stepped up onto the stage and, very gently, deposited Shantel onto her feet. Before she could even think about taking a step off the stage, and because I couldn't resist, I pulled her to me, and placed my lips on hers. Softly and gently, I moved my lips over hers. Her arms reached up and wrapped around me. She pressed her body against me. I deepened the kiss, and then shifted my stance a bit so there was a small bit of distance between us. This was not the time or place to get carried away. I moved my mouth away from hers and whispered against her check, "We will continue this later, Ms. Assistant. Lock me in."

"What's she doing?" Alex demanded. "And why were you kissing her?"

"She's locking me in," I told him. "Watch."

Shantel ran her fingers over the straight jacket's buckles, I ignored the kissing question. Alex is eight. I wasn't going to explain kissing to an eight-year-old.

"Where?" Shantel's hands roamed over the buckles.

I imagined those hands roaming all over me and I could barely speak. "Start at the back." I cleared my throat and stepped into the straight jacket. I wrapped my arms around myself in a self-hug. I remembered this part.

"This won't hurt?"

"Painless." I held very still as Shantel flipped each buckle closed.

"Now, Miss Assistant," I said. "I will get out of this straightjacket."

"What about me?" Alex stepped forward and stood on my foot. "What do I get to do?"

"Ouch!" I yelped sharply. "Go sit down."

"No," Alex crossed his hands over his chest. "She gets to be on stage."

"She is the Assistant," I growled.

Alex glared at me before he turned and stomped off the stage. He headed for the last seat in the house. I didn't care where he sat. I just wanted him off the stage. "Brothers," I mouthed to Shantel and shook my head. It seemed like a good idea to bring Alex, but that was before Shantel showed up. Now, I just wanted Shantel all to myself.

Shantel smiled, and I got lost in her smile. It's amazing how one minute, I was seeing clearly, and the next everything was hazy with a soft warm fuzz over it. It was better than any drug, and I wished I'd figured this out sooner. Find a girl you like, and get lost in her. Boom. Instant high.

I moved my arms inside the straight jacket and pushed against the heavy material. Immediately, I knew the trick was easier at twelve then at sixteen. I took a deep breath and tried to focus. I pictured myself maneuvering out of the jacket and dropping it to the ground. Dad always said the key to any magician's act was the ability to picture the result. Focus.

I pushed and strained against the jacket. The jacket wouldn't budge. I tried twisting and turning. The jacket remained locked in place. "I think I need some help," I mumbled.

Shantel stepped behind me and, with swift fingers, unbuckled the clasps. The jacket dropped to the stage with a heavy clunk. My insides felt the same way. Alex was awfully quiet. Surely, he should have been laughing and mocking me for failing at the trick. "Alex?" I swung around and looked out at empty seats.

I squinted at the lights and searched the theater.

There was no answer.

CHAPTER FIFTEEN

Shantel

Christopher raced all over the theater and yelled Alex's name. I calmly tried to show him the theater's back door was open. I said Alex probably went outside. But Christopher didn't want to listen. Instead, he looked like I was speaking a foreign language, and continued his mad dash around the theater. I'd never seen him so worked up, and it made me a little nervous. He seemed so irrational and out of control. I did not like irrational and out of control. Irrational and out of control reminded me of her. It reminded me of how sometimes for breakfast there would be cold soup instead of cold cereal, or how sometimes I'd come home from school to find every chair overturned, all the books pulled off the cases, and her car gone. No. I did not like irrational and out of control.

I had to get out of the theater. My chest felt tight, and my hands were clammy. I knew if I researched my symptoms, I would find the beginnings of a panic attack. So, I slipped out the back door and ran down the alley. Alex hadn't been gone that long and there weren't too many places he could go. I guessed he might be hungry and wandered down to the bakery. I was barely halfway down the alley when I saw him sitting at one of the black wrought iron tables outside the bakery. Mia stood next to him, and smiled. "I thought he'd like some sugar cookies."

"Good," Alex mumbled through a full mouth of blue sugar.

"Christopher is worried." I pulled out one of the black wrought iron chairs, and sat down opposite Alex. Worried seemed like a tiny word compared to what was happening in the theater. I wiped my hands on my skirt, and tried to resume breathing normally. A small band of sweat gathered on my forehead, and as discreetly as possible, I reached up and wiped it off.

"Get up," Christopher shouted from halfway down the alley.

I looked around wildly, and clutched the wrought iron chair. The iron hurt my hands, but I didn't let go. Did he want me to get up? I hadn't done anything wrong.

Christopher stormed down the alley. His face was a cold white sheet. When he reached us, he yanked Alex from the chair by his shoulders and held the boy like he was a bag of potatoes.

Alex squirmed and cried, but Christopher did not release him.

"We'll see you later," Christopher barked before heading toward the parking lot.

I stared after them, and crossed my hands over my chest to stop the shaking. It was like something took over Christopher and turned him from a rational, sane person, into this raving maniac lunatic. I didn't like this person at all.

"What is all the noise?" Mia wiped her hands on her apron.

"Christopher," I said and explained what happened.

Mia listened and then shook her head. "Are you sure about him? He sounds like he might have some other things going on," Mia paused. "I know your mom could be unreasonable, but not everyone is like that."

"Christopher is not like Mom," I said. "He was upset because Alex was missing. Everyone gets upset sometimes." I stopped to catch my breath. "He asked me to be his magician's assistant for the show."

Mia watched me before she said softly, "But you don't like magic."

"It'll be fine," I insisted. "I'm going to practice the tricks with him, and Gloria wants me to get a magician's assistant outfit. Something sexy don't you think?" I'd seen a show on

TV where the assistant was wearing a tight black, lacy body suit. The Magician couldn't keep his eyes off her.

"Well," Mia said slowly, "Assistants don't always have to be sexy."

"Yes," I insisted. "They do." Especially, when I had to compete with girls like Marissa who, I didn't doubt, would throw on a sexy magician's costume. "The boutique will have something."

Mia paused for a moment, before she said, "Give me a second to change."

I sank back against the wrought iron chair as Mia disappeared back into the bakery. I tapped my fingers on the table in a slow rhythm. I knew Christopher expected sexy. It was what someone like Marissa would wear. But, what would people think when they saw me? I was known as the Science Fair Champion. Newspaper articles filled a folder tucked into my desk drawer. What would happen when I changed into a Magician's Assistant wearing a sexy costume? What would Dad think when he saw me on stage in a sexy outfit with Christopher? He wouldn't think it was as great as me winning Science Fairs.

"Ready." Mia pulled the bakery door shut and stepped outside. Her hair was tied back with a red barrette and she had changed into a flowered summer skirt that swirled as we walked.

"You look great," I said truthfully. Mia always looked great. Even though she had a two-year-old, and seemed to work all the time, she always managed to look fabulous.

Mia pulled me close to her. "I could help you."

I frowned. "Is there something wrong with how I dress?"

Mia quickly shook her head. "I didn't mean it like that," she said. "I meant I could help you with Christopher."

Help me with Christopher. Why did Mia think I needed help with Christopher? I prided myself on not needing help with anything. Was it something I said? Something I did, which made Mia think I might need help? I'd worked so hard at the romance book club not to talk about Christopher. I hadn't joined in with the other ladies talking about their husbands and boyfriends. I pretended things were just like they always were with me. There was Drew who was just my science friend, and there were my science studies.

"I'm okay," I said slowly.

Mia slipped her arm into mine. "I know you are. You're always okay."

Something about how Mia said "you're always okay," made me cringe. It was as if "always being okay" was too safe. We walked past The Busy City Coffee shop. Drew sat at the counter in the front window. My physics books were piled high in front of him. As soon as he saw us, his face lit up, and he motioned for me to come inside.

"Oh no," I groaned.

"What?" Mia's gaze followed mine as Drew leaped up and headed toward the coffee shop door. "Oh," Mia said as she pulled me closer to her and whispered, "Let me take care of this."

Drew popped out of the shop and I inwardly shuddered. His dark hair was long and hung almost to his eyes. I never noticed how badly he needed a haircut. His plaid shirt was untucked and wrinkled. Christopher's shirts were never wrinkled. His jeans were clean, and, half the time, the back of his short hair was still damp from a shower. Plus, he always smelled wonderful. Now that I thought about it, Drew never smelled good. And, immediately, I felt bad. I shouldn't even be thinking about things like smells, hair, and clothes.

"The books are great," Drew gushed. "You should come in. We can talk about some of them. I'll buy you a coffee." He smiled shyly at me.

My stomach churned. That smile. I'd never seen Drew look at me like that before. Well, maybe he had been looking at me like that for a long time, and I just hadn't wanted to see it. The way his eyes sparkled, the way his ears turned red. And suddenly, I felt sick. Why did things have to get complicated? Why did they have to change?

"She'd love to have coffee, but she has to help me," Mia

said quickly. "I've got to have the perfect dress for this party on Saturday." Mia tossed back her head and laughed gaily. "You know me, I'm always putting things off to the last minute."

A shadow of confusion crossed Drew's face. "I didn't know you liked shopping,"

"Well..." I struggled to come up with an answer. It was true I didn't like shopping. I didn't pour over the latest fashion magazines. Sometimes I picked out something special at the Boutique, but most of the time, I wore jeans and a t-shirt with one of my scarves. It hadn't really mattered until now.

"Okay," Drew said quietly without waiting for me to explain. "Maybe another time."

"I'm sorry, Drew." I touched his arm. Drew had been my friend for years. We'd gone to every science fair competition together since we were in sixth grade. There had never been anything between us. Well, as far as I could remember, there had never been anything between us. But, maybe everyone kept secrets. Maybe everyone had one thing they didn't want to talk about, and kept it hidden away. Maybe life was like physics, and Drew and I saw totally different realities. "We'll talk about the books later, okay?"

I wanted to keep apologizing. But I didn't quite know for what or how. I was sorry things were changing. I was sorry I couldn't stay and be like I always had been. I was sorry, but I didn't know how to stop the change. And, I did not want to stop what was happening with Christopher. Even if he did get a little manic when Alex disappeared, and even if he did seem a little moody sometimes, I was beginning to realize I liked the complexities. He was an equation I could never quite figure out, and I liked that.

"Ready?" Mia asked as she gently pulled me away from Drew.

"Sure," I said and smiled apologetically to Drew. I let Mia lead me down the street to Monique's Boutique.

Two stores later, I pulled open the door and a small bell chimed above my head.

It didn't take long for Mia to find a long, black dress with sequins. She held it up.

"Perfect!" she exclaimed. "Try it on, Shantel."

"It's a magic show," I said. "Not a black tie event." I shivered in the way that happened when people said someone walked over your grave. I was standing in the Boutique shop and I was looking for an outfit to wear to perform in a magic show. I didn't like magic because bad things happened, but now, here I was, about to perform in the magic show.

I drifted away from Mia and headed toward the back of the small consignment shop. I stopped in front of a rack of shoes. I loved shoes. I had three pairs of boots all embroidered in different patterns. None of them were practical for our wet, Pacific Northwest winters, but I loved all of them. I picked up a pair of high black heels and held one up to my left foot. They were higher than anything I'd ever owned. But, I was short next to Christopher. I could get away with very high heels as long as I practiced beforehand.

"I'll be right back," Mia said from behind me.

She held a stack of lacy garments and darted into the dressing room. It must be easy to be married, I thought. She could wear all the lacy lingerie she wanted, and not worry about if it was the right thing or not.

Tentatively, I wandered over to the lingerie rack. I always bought sensible pairs of underwear and bras. It was something I never thought about until Christopher's hands found their way to my sensible underwear. Did other girls he'd been with wear the silky lace black ones? My stomach turned over in small butterflies. I remembered the way it felt to be with Christopher in the hammock. Maybe, I should look a little harder at this rack of clothes.

As I combed through the lacy nightgowns, my face felt like it was on fire, and everyone could see why I was looking in this rack. Carefully, I searched through lacy bras as Mia emerged from the small dressing room. Her face was scrunched into a frown. "You just lose everything with a baby," she muttered. She replaced the black nightgown on a small shelf.

"Find anything?" Mia asked, and smiled. "I don't think

you're looking in the right place."

I ignored Mia and moved aside black lacy tops. I had to find something. Didn't she understand? Didn't she know about girls like Marissa, or guys like Christopher, who were experienced and expected things? Christopher would expect me to have a sexy costume. I stopped at a lacy top with a scoop neckline. A piece of black cloth covered the inside and as I held it up to the light, I knew my skin wouldn't show through the lace except on the arms. It might work with jeans. It was sexy, but not too sexy. Tentatively, I held the top up to my face. I turned around to face a small mirror attached to a post. Would Christopher see something in me with this outfit? Would something in this outfit give me confidence like Marissa? Would I be able to run my fingers up and over his lips and make his face turn all red? Did I have that kind of power?

Mia stepped up behind me. "It's a nice top," she said and lifted my hair on top of my head. "Wear it like this." She smiled at me. "Shows off your neckline. Just like your Mom."

For a minute, I couldn't breathe. I didn't want to think about Mom. Keep it together. I told myself. You can control this. You don't have to think about her. Not now. I clutched the dress into my arms and scooped up a pair of high heels in a size 7. I walked away from Mia and dumped it all on the counter. I dug into my purse and pulled out my wallet. Mia pushed me gently out of the way.

"No, no. I've got it. Your Mom would like that." She frowned at the shoes. "These too?"

"Yes," I said firmly. I had to have the shoes. The shoes were what made the costume sexy.

"Mmm…." Mia bit her lip, but didn't say anything else.

Monique rang up the purchase, wrapped the top in white tissue paper, and slipped it all into a large pink shopping bag with small plastic handles…even the shoes. Thanking Mia, I picked up the shopping bag and pushed open the door. I wanted to get out of the shop that had suddenly become very hot. But, as soon as I opened the door, I wished I'd stayed inside a little longer.

"Shantel," Kathi called as she hurried across the empty street, followed by Dad. "There you are! I waited for you, but your Dad stopped by, and I closed the shop to take a lunch break."

The yarn shop! I'd forgotten all about the yarn shop. Everything happened so fast. Christopher. Alex. Shopping with Mia. "I'm so sorry," I said. "I forgot. It was busy this morning and—" I stopped and stared at the large folder under Dad's arm with the bank emblem. "What's that?"

"The farm, "Dad said quietly. "The farm is going into foreclosure."

"The letter," I exclaimed. Where was the letter? I searched my purse. Had Dad found the letter?

"They sent it to my office. Registered mail. I already knew."

I felt like I was going to be sick. He already knew? And he hadn't told me? The whole world swirled around me. Dad and I were a team. Dad and I had always been a team. When Mom had her bad days, Dad always took me to someplace special. Sometimes it was a museum, sometimes we went on a hike, but it was always Dad and I.

"What's in the bag?" Dad eyed the pink, plastic sack.

"A shirt," I didn't look Dad in the eye and clutched the bag to my chest.

CHAPTER SIXTEEN

Christopher

Sunday night, I couldn't sleep. I kicked the sheets off and tossed onto my side. I kept thinking about Alex. How it felt to look out into that empty theater and find him gone. Vanished. The panic and the fear rose up in me like a monster. And to be honest, I realized something was changing. I always just thought about me. Me and what I needed. It was part of what the guys at the Meeting called the disease. The addict always thinks about himself, and how to get that next high. But now, things were shifting and moving around. There was Alex. There was Mom. There was Shantel. There was Dad. And, there was the magic show— I had to figure out how to do Dad's tricks without him here to show me. My head hurt just thinking about all of it.

I wasn't going to fall asleep with this much on my mind. I flipped on the light and yanked my Big Book off the dresser shelf. I didn't feel okay in my skin. The alarm clock glowed 3:00 a.m.. Charlie always said I could call him any time, but it seemed so stupid to say I was feeling funny. I wasn't at a party or something. I was home. In my bed. But my mind just wouldn't shut off.

I flipped through the Big Book and tried to figure out what I was supposed to read. None of what was in the book dealt with girls, or little brothers, or magic shows. It was more about drinking and that wasn't my problem. Drugs were the problem.

I tossed the book on the floor. It landed face down and I swung my legs out of bed. I grabbed a t-shirt and shorts out of the dresser. I needed to take a good jog to clear my head. Silently, I crept out of my room and down the stairs. Quickly, I checked the white panel on the wall to see if Mom set the alarm. The screen blinked and I punched in the code. I waited until the silence alarms sign flashed. More than a couple times, I came home stoned out of my mind, and set off the stupid alarm. Another advantage to sobriety, I smiled to myself. No alarms in the middle of the night.

Once outside, I inhaled the cool summer night air. I'd been awake a lot at three a.m. when I used. But I'd never noticed the clean crisp smell of the air, or the way the light breeze silently rustled through the leaves. Turning left, I jogged down the street, hoping that maybe, just maybe, I could run away this uncomfortable space inside me.

I ran hard, but it didn't take me long to realize that I was headed directly to Michael's. I didn't purposely go this direction, did I? Did I subconsciously want to see if he might be around? Slowing, I passed his house. A small porch light glowed, and a lamp from inside the house shone onto the front porch.

I stared up at his bedroom window.

Dark.

Michael's small, beat up Honda, with the shiny wheels and tinted windows, was parked in the back of the driveway.

Tonight Michael was home.

Asleep.

A good thing for me.

I turned and headed away from Michael's house. My feet hit the pavement.

Hard.

I ran faster and faster for thirty minutes until I reached home again. This time, when I dropped exhausted into bed, I didn't think about anything until four hours later when my alarm buzzed. Groaning, I hustled into the shower and swore not to do the three a.m. running stunt again.

For the last two weeks, I attended a sunrise AA Meeting and then headed over to physics class a little early. If I got to class early, I could get the night's homework done plus extra reading. I guess I must kinda like physics. McCallister never arrives until five minutes before class, but a secretary would unlock the door for me. Everyone smiled at me. They appeared happy to see a new me.

I was beginning to think I was happy to be a new me, too.

But, this morning, McCallister was ahead of me and the classroom door was wide-open. As soon as I walked in, she smirked at me. She dropped the local paper on my desk. "Looks like someone is famous."

I gritted my teeth. It took a lot not to react to her. I had a small nagging feeling of what it may have been like for the people around me when I was using.

I glanced at the paper. It was the story about Dad and underneath it, an article about me performing at the theater. My stomach felt like I'd eaten rocks for breakfast as I read:

Christopher Parks, teen magician will perform on Saturday as a part of the Riverview Theater Annual Fundraiser. Unlike many teen magician's, Christopher has a secret up his sleeve that is a little more than magical. Christopher was trained under his father, William Parks. Parks was the town's magician for years, until the magic caught up with him and he was recently arrested for embezzlement. Now, his son will begin a new generation of Magicians. The town awaits to see what this new magician will have up his sleeve.

Embezzlement. Dad was arrested for embezzlement. It was the first I heard of his charge. Mom wouldn't talk, but now it didn't matter. I think I suspected all along. All those fancy trips. New carpet. New furniture. Sure, they are things we could have done at one point when Mom's real estate career was booming, but houses weren't selling, and Dad's accounting job didn't pay that well.

"Trouble?" Marissa asked as she slid into the seat next to me. Her heavy perfume made me inhale sharply and pray for fresh air. I was glad Shantel didn't take a bath in heavy lotions or scents.

"No more than usual." I touched the side of her dark

sunglasses. "Might want to take these off." Wearing dark sunglasses inside was something I tried once and never tried again. Sunglasses are a dead giveaway for red-rimmed eyes from too much doping the night, or sometimes morning, before. McCallister wasn't dumb. Once she saw Marissa with the sunglasses, she would be all over her.

Marissa sniffed and hunted around in her large leather bag for a Kleenex. She didn't remove the sunglasses.

"What's going on?"

"Can you take me to an appointment this afternoon?"

"Where?"

"Planned Parenthood."

"Whoa!" I leaned back in my chair. I've taken Marissa to a lot of appointments. She has a driver's license, but without a car, she relied on Michael and me. Michael isn't too dependable with the big things, so she usually called me in as a back-up. To me, it seemed like Marissa had a lot of appointments. Hair. Nail fix-ups or something. Even a couple for doctor appointments. Marissa had a lot of miscellaneous illnesses that checked out wrong. But Planned Parenthood? No, that was off my list.

"Don't you have a girlfriend to take you?"

I didn't ask about Michael. I was pretty sure he didn't know anything. Whatever was wrong, Marissa would take care of things. That was one thing I liked about her. Marissa was a survivor, a girl who knew how to get things done. Sure, sometimes she had to manipulate the situation a little bit, but she could take care of problems all on her own.

Marissa sniffed harder. She wiped the Kleenex under her sunglasses and dabbed at the tears which rolled down her cheeks. The sunglasses weren't about a night of heavy using, but more like a heavy night of tears. Marisa blew her nose, and pulled away the Kleenex. A huge glob of heavy, black mascara covered the tissue.

"Girls talk." She sniffed again. "Please. I need you there."

I softened. This was the agreement Marissa and I had. She needed me to be there for her. Michael rarely was, and so she relied on me. Marissa lived with her dad and he was often gone. He worked the late shift at a gas station, and they didn't have a lot of money. Marissa had attached herself to Michael in ninth grade. She seemed oblivious to his drugging or how it affected her. It was something I didn't really pay attention to when I was using myself, but now everything seemed to be getting clearer.

I wasn't going to let her down. I would figure out a way to talk to her about Michael. "I'll take you," I said. "No worries."

CHAPTER SEVENTEEN

Shantel

The storm hit without warning. It was a saying Mom liked. No one ever mentioned that often, she could be the storm that hit without warning. The one time we could guarantee a storm would not hit was when Mom paid bills. Unlike other people who seemed to get stressed about money, Mom took it as a challenge. Each month, no matter if she was having a good day or not, she'd spread the bills out in front of her and punch numbers into the small calculator. Sometimes the rows and rows of strawberries and blueberries didn't produce enough to sell. But, Mom always found a way to make it work. She'd go into the barn, and pull out some antique she'd found at a flea market, or old picture that looked like it wasn't worth anything. Then, she'd leave for a couple hours, and when she'd come back, she'd hand Dad a deposit slip and say, "Everything is taken care of."

I wished I had a little bit more of Mom's ability to weather storms.

On Monday afternoon, I lay on the flat board on the theater's stage floor. The board was smooth under my palms, and legs. My feet were inside the silver shackles. When I turned my head, I could see Gloria showing a stage hand how to paint a deep, rich blue dresser. At the same time, she was shouting out instructions to a small group doing improv by the door.

And then there was Marissa. Who could miss her? She was sitting in the front row wearing another one of her crop tops that showed her middle and the tattoo. Today, she had on thin strappy sandals with at least a three inch heel, and her finger nails were painted a bright pink. She sat on the edge of the seat, one hand checking her cell phone every few seconds, while she barked out instructions to Christopher on how he was standing with his back to the audience. Even from the stage, I could smell her thick perfume.

"Shantel," Christopher said. "Are you paying attention?"

"Yes." I drew my gaze away from Marissa and turned my head so I could look straight up at the ceiling. The stage lights hurt my eyes, and I closed them against the bright white light. My eyes already hurt with all the crying I'd done in the last two days about the farm. Dad said there was nothing we could do. The bank was letting us live on the farm through the summer and the berry season, and then we'd have to go. He would get us an apartment in town, and I could finish my last two years of high school. Dad said I didn't need to worry about anything, all the finances and paperwork had been turned over to the bank. But, it felt like something had been taken away inside of me, leaving me with a large empty hole.

To add to everything else going wrong, Christopher was forty-five minutes late to practice. I was about to leave but Gloria insisted she needed help with the performance flyer, and I was the only one who could do graphics as well as get everyone's name spelled correctly.

The whole time I worked on the flyer, I kept looking at the small clock on the computer, watching as each minute ticked by. I finished the flyer and was ready to leave, when Christopher rushed into the theater with Marissa in tow. Gloria raised an eyebrow and informed him audience members were not allowed. Christopher stepped up next to Gloria and said something which made her face soften and she relented. "Well, okay, then, but make sure she stays off the stage."

He didn't ask me if I wanted Marissa to be there.

"When I raise the cover of the box," Christopher instructed. "Move quickly. You'll slide your feet out of the shackles, and curl up into a ball in the front part of the box." He frowned.

"At least that's what I think happens."

I wiggled my feet. To the audience, it appeared I was caught in the silver shackles. But, I knew there was plenty of room for me to easily get my feet out. The problem was something seemed to be wrong with all of Christopher's tricks. A piece was missing from each one of them. He kept telling me not to worry. But I was worried. We only had a few days before the performance, and it seemed the tricks were still pretty rough. I wanted one thing this summer to go right. Just one thing.

I tucked and curled my legs into a ball. "Is this right?"

"Yes." Christopher tapped the middle of the box. "I will slide the sword here. But if it misses," he slid his fingers along the edges, "the sword is plastic. It won't hurt you."

He kept telling me the sword couldn't hurt me every time we did the trick. I finally asked him if there was another trick with a real sword. Christopher had gotten real quiet, and then said, "Yes." And nothing more.

"Chris?" Marissa whined. "Can you take me home? I don't feel very good."

I slipped my feet out of the shackles, and raised myself to a sitting position. "We're practicing," I said firmly. "We have to get these tricks mastered. The show is only two days away." Under my breath I added, "And his name is Christopher. Not Chris."

"But I don't feel good." Marissa rubbed her stomach. Her silver bracelet moved up and down on her arm. "Please, Chris."

I waited for Christopher to say something. Why didn't he tell her we were practicing and she had to wait? Instead, he pulled out his car keys, and muttered, "Sorry. I'll be back in a second."

Fuming, I stood up as he positioned his hand under Marissa's elbow. Without looking at me, he guided her up the aisle like she was feeble. I clenched my fists. She hadn't seemed feeble to me in physics that morning. I'd arrived to class a few minutes early and found Marissa sitting at the lab table next to Christopher. She was running her fingertips over his arm and looking deep into his eyes. He hadn't even noticed me until I sat down at the table in front of them, and dropped my book on the ground accidentally. My stomach felt like a boulder was inside. What would make Christopher tell Marissa to go away?

I walked over and picked up one of the yellow programs from an empty front row seat. Gloria had just run a few sample copies so I could look them over and proof them. I had been so excited to write our names together. Christopher Parks, Magician Performing with Shantel Lovelace, Assistant. It did not say, Christopher Parks and Marissa Evans. It said, Shantel Lovelace.

I ran my finger down the list of names, carefully checking each one for spelling errors. Most of the acts were names I recognized. After summer camp, and theater classes, everyone poured into the bakery for snacks. Mia and I knew everyone who was performing in the theater.

Christopher and I were the last performance. We were the grand finale, the showstopper, the act that would encourage everyone to open their wallets and contribute to the theater. Gloria said people loved William Parks. Everyone was excited to see the magic tradition continue with his son. Christopher looked a little green when she said the part about his dad, but quickly shrugged it off and said, "It'll be good."

But this whole thing with Marissa was not "good."

"Shantel," Christopher's warm voice said from behind me. "I thought you left."

"I'll be back." His eyes searched mine. "Okay?"

There was a raging storm of emotion inside me. I wanted to trust him. But, one part of me argued the facts were obvious. Christopher spent a lot of time with Marissa. He liked when she ran her fingers over his lips. He liked talking to her in physics, and he had obviously been somewhere with her this afternoon. He'd forgotten about the time and was late to practice. Now, he was taking her home. How could I trust him?

Marissa did look sick. I peered shyly at him, and he was gazing at me with such concern it made me really want to believe him. I fumbled with the program in my hand. The pages fluttered as I felt the two sides battling inside me.

"Christopher," Marissa pleaded.

"Coming." Christopher squeezed my arm. He gave me another one of those looks which made me melt. Then, he turned and jumped off the stage in a large, hurdle leap. I stood, watching them leave, until Gloria touched my arm. "Can I talk to you?"

"Mmm..." I peeled my eyes from Christopher's back.

"The theater's money box has disappeared."

"What?" Startled, I turned to face Gloria.

The theater kept a box of money at the front window for ticket sales. The box was usually locked and no one had the key except Gloria.

"Saturday," Gloria said very slowly. "Christopher was here. You saw him. You came to give me the book."

"Christopher didn't do it!"

Gloria stared deeply into my eyes. "He was the only one in the theater. The money was gone afterwards. Unless..." she searched my face, "...you took it for some reason?"

"No," I whispered.

"I didn't think so."

I felt like I'd just been kicked in the stomach.

CHAPTER EIGHTEEN

Christopher

I parked the truck in the empty theater parking lot. It took a long time to get Marissa home. She had to stop at the pharmacy to pick up a few things. Afterward, she'd wanted to drive by Michael's house. Just to see if he was home. Which of course, he wasn't. So then she wanted to wait a few minutes to see if he might come home. Which of course, he didn't, and a few minutes turned into plenty of minutes. By the time I finally dropped Marissa at her house, and drove back to the theater, I knew I needed to not only find Shantel, but also get over to the AA Meeting which had already started. Being around Marissa made me realize how crazy the addiction could get—to drugs or people.

A small gold light shone from the bakery windows. The door was open and light jazz drifted down the alley. I quickly headed over and knocked on the back door. Mia answered, her hair pulled into a fishnet and flour decorated her cheeks.

"Shantel is at the yarn shop," Mia said.

I was off like a flash. I knew the yarn shop. I'd stopped in to ask about fixing Shantel's loom. The shop was empty that day. Tonight, there was a small group of ladies gathered in a circle. Shantel was bent over a table loom and patiently showing another woman something about her warp.

"Hey," I said softly. I didn't want to interrupt, but I was curious about what she was doing with the yarn and the loom.

Shantel gave me a small curt nod and went back to threading the loom. My gut pinched with anxiety. I knew she wasn't happy about Marissa, but I didn't know how to explain my loyalty to Michael's girlfriend. It was something I had to work out.

Shantel slowly threaded a light blue piece of yarn through a small wire eyelet in the back of the loom. When she finished, she handed the yarn to the woman, and made small corrections in the threading. Finally she turned and looked up at me. I was sunk. I wanted to make it up to her and take her somewhere nice, but I had to go to a Meeting.

"I gotta get to a Meeting," I said quickly. And then, because I did want to spend time with her, I asked, "Wanna come?"

On Friday nights, the AA Meeting turned into an Open Meeting. Which meant friends and family could attend and listen to us talk about our stories. The old timers said Open Meetings help friends and family understand us a bit more. I wanted Shantel to understand me. But my hands were sweating like it was game day. Would Shantel want to go? Or would she give me the same answer as Mom? Sobriety was my problem and not hers.

Shantel raised one eyebrow. Then, in a very noncommittal voice, she said, "It'd be interesting."

"Interesting," I repeated. The grin spread across my face. Interesting wasn't really the word I would use to describe the guys who got up and talked about what they'd done when they were using. More like entertaining with a bit of sobering reality at the end.

Shantel gave the loom woman a few more instructions. I leaned against a wood shelf and prepared myself to wait like I had been doing all day for Marissa. But Shantel wasn't Marissa. She relayed one more thing to loom woman, grabbed her purse, waved good-bye to the yarn circle group, and said, "Well? Aren't we going?"

"Yes!" I hopped over a stack of yarn and followed her out the door, but not before I caught more than one lady in the yarn circle smiling at me. I felt good. I had been given the yarn circle thumbs up. I had to hurry to catch up to Shantel. She was already headed at a fast clip down the street to where I could see a full church parking lot.

"Are we late?" She asked.

"A little." I picked up Shantel's hand and linked her fingers with mine. She didn't respond and her hand was cold. I was just so grateful to have a "friends and family" member with me. I squeezed Shantel's hand, but it hung limply and I wondered if maybe I totally misjudged the whole situation. It wouldn't be the first time.

Inside the church, the scent of strong coffee and laughter rose from the basement room. I picked up my step. If we hurried, we could slip in during the midst of the laughter. I strutted into the room, walking a bit like a peacock. Smart, sexy Shantel was holding my hand. Even if it was a bit limp, I felt this was the moment I had been waiting for during all those awful days in rehab. The days when everything felt big, black, and dark and the counselors kept promising a better tomorrow. Finally, I had my better tomorrow!

The room was packed. There was one open metal folding chair in the back of the room. I headed toward it. Shantel could have the chair and I would stand behind her. I could lean against the wall where there were already a couple guys standing.

"And now it's time for open sharing," Mike announced from the small, wood podium. "I'd like to open the meeting up by calling on Christopher."

I gently guided Shantel to the chair and tried to swallow the large lump lodged in my throat. Why is Mike calling on me? I obviously missed the beginning of the Meeting. I had no idea if there was a topic. Were we talking about a Step or a chapter in the Big Book? Was this open sharing where I was supposed to share my life story? My stomach tensed. Was the guy trying to call me out? Embarrass me in front of everyone? I never saw guys fight in an AA meeting, or afterward. But right now, I wanted to pull the guy aside and give him a big wallop.

"Christopher!" Mike's voice boomed from the small microphone on the podium.

No. I wanted to say. I don't want to share. I met Charlie's eyes across the room. I didn't have a choice. I had to step to the microphone. "I'll share." I tried to sound pleasant. I headed toward the front of the room and prayed my thoughts would gather themselves together. I remembered other guys who shared. There was always something about being grateful for sobriety. I could say a few words about what it had been like while using. Although I wasn't too sure I wanted to share that part. Telling my using story felt a little vulnerable with Shantel listening. It wasn't a pretty story—passed out on park benches, waking up to find myself drenched and cold as I stumbled home, lying to Mom and hoping she didn't notice my empty bed. And that was just what I remembered. There was a whole lot I didn't remember.

I stepped up to the podium and Mike thumped me on the shoulder. The sea of faces stared back at me, and I fought down the nausea. I never had a problem performing in front of people. But performing on-stage or in a school hallway with magic tricks wasn't the same as standing up and talking about your feelings in an AA Meeting. Performance was about taking on the personality of someone else. Standing in front of the AA Meeting was about trying to figure out how to drop all those personalities and be real.

"Evening." I clutched the edges of the wood podium. I hoped my voice wasn't shaking too badly. "I'd like to thank my sponsor." I looked toward the back left corner. "For helping me." Charlie nodded gravely and gave me the thumbs-up signal. "And," I turned and nodded to Shantel, "I'd like to thank my girl for putting up with me so far." I burst with pride at that comment. Shantel's face turned bright red. She looked like she wanted to sink through a trap door in the floor.

"I was just a kid who liked to get high," I started. "And I got caught. Bad caught." I took a large swallow and stared at the podium. The day Coach pulled me into his office and said it was my turn for the pee test. I'd been out using all night. My eyes were still blood shot. But I had no choice. I peed in that small cup and with each drop another person lost their belief in me.

"I'm an addict," I said loudly into the microphone. "An addict." I'd admitted the words a bunch of different times. I told groups at the treatment center. I told Charlie and of course when I say my name at Meetings. "Hi, I'm Christopher, and I'm an addict." But it was different up at the podium with all the eyes looking at me. I was vulnerable.

Exposed.

Raw.

I turned to Mike. "I think I'm done now. That okay?"

"Course!" Mike stepped forward. He pulled me close in a large hug that made me say, "Oof."

"You keep coming back!" Mike patted me on the back.

I nodded briefly and stepped away from the podium. I made my way to the back of the room and stood behind Shantel's chair. She turned slightly and slipped her hand into mine. Her hand gripped mine, warm and solid.

CHAPTER NINETEEN

Shantel

Christopher sat down and I pretended I heard everything he said. I slipped my hand into his and leaned against him. I hoped he didn't ask me anything about his talk. There were so many thoughts running around my head it was impossible to listen to him.

After the meeting ended, Christopher introduced me to an older man named Charlie. Charlie wore jeans and a flannel shirt. He towered over me, and talked in a loud, deep voice. I didn't like Charlie. It felt as if Charlie could see through me, and he didn't like what he saw. I quickly excused myself and went to get a piece of the thick, white birthday cake with pink and yellow frosting. Christopher explained birthday cake was for the AA birthdays, not belly button birthdays. The cake wasn't as good as Mia's bakery cake, and I could tell it came from a supermarket. A large cake box with a plastic see through lid sat in the trash can. I took a bite from my plastic fork. The frosting had that rich and gooey taste which would never have come from Mia's bakery. But I ate every bite and pretended all the loud chatter around me about Steps and staying sober was something I enjoyed.

Finally, the last coffee pot was put away, the last chair folded, and the last AA pamphlet placed in a box. Christopher suggested we go over to a small park bench across the street from the church. The park overlooked the slow, meandering river. In the late summer evening, the sky glowed a soft, rosy pink. It sounded like a perfect idea.

Christopher and I walked slowly toward the park. He held my hand, and I matched my step to his. When we reached the bench, he pulled me down beside him. "Dad used to like this park," he said. "Everything…" his voice took on a hard edge. "Everything was my fault."

"Your fault?"

Christopher rubbed small circles on my left arm. His words rushed out. "Rehab is expensive. Dad wanted to me to have a good place. I know he stole money so I could go to rehab."

Christopher's voice cracked, and I wound my fingers through his. "It wasn't your fault," I said. My words didn't help him, and so I did the only thing I could think of. I leaned forward and placed my lips on his. I kissed Christopher until I felt his arms wrap around me, and he pulled me so I was sitting half on-top of him.

I felt confident and, leaning back to touch his mouth, I ran my finger along his lips the way I'd seen Marissa do. Over his lips and then I traced a line down along his jaw bone before I covered his mouth with mine. I felt like I was drowning in Christopher's kiss.

"Want to go somewhere else?" I asked. My heart pounded.

Christopher took his lips off mine, and looked into my eyes. "I know a way into the theater," he murmured.

"The theater?"

"Yes." Christopher gave me that slow, sexy smile. "If you want to go somewhere else."

"Perfect." I hoped my voice wasn't shaking or that Christopher could tell I was starting to sweat under my arms. I stood and Christopher popped off the bench like he couldn't wait to get moving. My hands were clammy, and my breathing increased. Pretend, I insisted to myself. Pretend you know exactly what you are doing. Pretend.

But the pretend game wasn't working. I couldn't settle down. How was I supposed to pretend when I didn't know what I was doing? I walked beside Christopher across the street and down two blocks the theater. Our feet clicked on the sidewalk, and in the dark night, the noise sounded like a thousand tap shoes. I was sure everyone would hear us. People would come from miles around and say, "We know where you are going and why!"

The street was deserted and all the shops had their small window lights illuminated. There weren't even any cars that passed us. Once the AA Meeting emptied out, Main Street was dead quiet. The night air was cool on my hot cheeks. Could Christopher hear how fast my heart was pounding in the still night? When we reached the brick theater, Christopher motioned for me to follow him around to the back.

At the theater's back door, Christopher reached into a small row of bricks and pulled out a key. He waved it in the air in a grand flourish.

"A key?" In all the time I'd known Gloria, she'd never told me about the key.

"Dad hid it," Christopher said, and smiled.

"Dad was always forgetting his theater key. He got tired of calling Gloria and asking her to let him in for practice. He finally made an extra one and kept it here."

Christopher slipped the key into the theater lock and pushed open the door. I knew there wouldn't be any alarms. Security systems and cameras were not something the theater could afford. And who would want to break into the theater anyway?

Christopher took my hand, and we stepped inside. As my eyes adjusted to the dark, I heard creaks and groans I never heard during the day. It seemed a little spooky, and I wasn't sure the theater was such a good idea. But before I could say anything, Christopher slipped my arm through his, and pulling me close said, "Come on."

"Where are we going?" There was panic in my voice. We were inside the dark theater. There was no one here. No one at all. What had I gotten myself into?

"The orchestra pit," Christopher said softly against my left cheek. "It'll be nice there."

I swallowed hard. Gloria stored the costumes in the orchestra pit. I'd once offered to help Gloria organize the costumes. We could box things up. All the dresses could be hung on a rack. It wouldn't be hard to install a clothing rack in the pit. We could find old hangers at the thrift store. But, Gloria shrugged me off, and said half the fun of the orchestra pit was trying to find the right outfit. It was like a game. You never knew what you were going to find. I'd never told Gloria, or anyone else, that I'd seen a ghost in the orchestra pit. He'd come out when I was sorting through old pioneer clothes, dropping bonnets in one box, and long skirts in another. I couldn't talk to him. Above me, I heard people breaking down the sets, and I knew if I started talking to the ghost, everyone would think I was crazy. Just like Mom.

Instead, I'd simply stared at the ghost. He had put his hand to his lips, mouthed "Shhh" at me, and then disappeared. After that, I made sure not to go into the orchestra pit.

And now, Christopher and I were going to be alone in the theater. Alone in the orchestra pit with the ghost.

"Wait!" I said, and darted off to where I knew the props were kept for the upcoming talent show. I opened the box, and dug through hula hoops, dancing shoes, and a plastic ukulele. I kept digging until my hands felt the small, plastic flameless candle. It was a part of the set for a comedy show that took place in a restaurant. Jake, the town's comedian, had argued with Gloria about his set. She'd told him it was a talent show, and all he needed to do was get up to the mic and do his comedy routine. But, Jake had insisted he needed to create atmosphere. He said he wanted a real-life comedy situation, and he was going to set up small tables with the flameless candles. He'd ask audience members to come up on stage and be a part of his act. Jake thought it was genius. Gloria thought it was too much of an effort. She'd finally given in and placed his act right before intermission. She told him all of his set had to be off stage by the time intermission was over.

"Here." I grabbed two of the plastic candles. I handed one to Christopher. At least, maybe the ghost would see our lights, and go away.

Slowly we made our way around the darkened stage and

toward the front of the theater. "How are we going to get down there?" I asked. The stage pit had a separate door, and I was pretty sure that different keys fit different doors. Gloria kept a bunch of keys on a round ring which jingled in her pocket.

"Jump." Christopher leaned over the orchestra pit, and placed his weight on his hands. He peered over the edge. "It's not that far. We can easily swing our legs over the ledge, like this." Christopher dropped one leg over the railing, and then the other. With the ease of an agile athlete, he jumped into the pit.

"Come on." He fluffed the clothes around him. "Nothing to fear."

I looked down into the pit. I was shorter than Christopher so my leap was going to be a longer stretch. I leaned on the railing and tried to see into the dark shadows around Christopher. Was the ghost hanging out in the shadows?

Something creaked behind me, and I jumped.

"Scared?" Christopher's deep laugh filled the empty theater.

"No," I said, as trembling, I swung my leg over the railing. Once I was balanced, I swung the other leg, and then peered into the dark space below me. It'd just be like jumping out of the barn into the hay. Only instead of hay, it'd be the soft clothes which would break my fall.

I closed my eyes, and pushed against the railing. All sense of safety left me, as I flew through the air.

But instead of hitting soft clothing, I hit a solid body, and the next thing I knew, Christopher and I were in the middle of all those poofy clothes.

"Pretty good," Christopher whispered as he wrapped his arms around me. I lay next to him and tried to relax. There was no noise but the sound of us breathing.

Christopher's arms went slack around me. "Christopher," I said, hesitantly. "What's wrong?"

"Nothing." All the playfulness was drained from his voice.

I absently played with a small lace collar. What was wrong with Christopher? Was it something about me? Had

Christopher changed his mind? Or, I listened to my beating heart, was Christopher afraid? It'd never occurred to me Christopher might be afraid. But maybe he was scared, just like me.

"Christopher," I said softly.

"Mmm…."

"You're sure nothing's wrong?"

"No," Christopher said. This time his voice cracked.

I picked up the scratchy fabric of a fluffy dress. I ran it between my fingers. So, maybe nothing was going to happen. That was okay with me. It was more than okay with me.

I twirled the fluffy dress between my fingers. There was something I had to tell Christopher, and right now, lying in the dark, when I couldn't see his expression, seemed like a good time. "Gloria said that someone stole the theater's ticket money," I said carefully.

"What?" Christopher turned around to face me. I could make out the outline of his narrow face in the dark. His hair was tousled and stuck out in the back. I resisted the urged to reach out and smooth it down.

"She said it happened while we were practicing on Saturday."

"She thinks it was me."

"Yes," I said softly.

Christopher swore. "Everyone thinks I'm just like Dad."

"It's not that," I protested. "We were the only ones in the theater. The money was gone after we left."

"We're the only ones here now," Christopher said. "Maybe we could make the money reappear?"

And suddenly, he rolled over, and stared hard at me

CHAPTER TWENTY

Christopher

After I dropped Shantel off at her farm, I drove slowly toward home. I'd felt so good at the Meeting. And then, afterward, on the bench, when I started talking about Dad, I had gotten that terrible feeling again. The feeling I'd had since his arrest. It was my fault. Dad never would have stolen that money if it wasn't for me going to rehab. And when Shantel suggested we go somewhere, I wanted to do anything to run away from those feelings. I knew the key would still be there. I remembered the day Dad hid it. He liked to practice early in the morning or on Sunday afternoons. Gloria said she didn't care, just as long as he remembered to lock everything up. It was probably about the third time we'd stood out in the wind and the rain waiting for Gloria to unlock the theater. She hadn't looked too happy when she arrived. She and Dad had some sharp words, and the next thing I knew, Dad was hauling me off to the hardware   store across town to get another key made.

Once Shantel and I got into the theater, I'd suddenly realized where she expected things to go. And that freaked me out. By the time we got into the orchestra pit, it was all I could do not to bolt. Sure, I'd had lots of experience when I was using. But, I didn't remember a lot of it, and the times I did remember, I'd been high. The pills made me feel like I was invincible and could do anything. Lying there with Shantel, I'd felt like I was in seventh grade getting my first kiss. It scared me.

If I had a couple minutes, I could have gotten over the fear. At least to continue a little bit of what we were doing on the bench. But then, she told me about Gloria and the money box.

I shook my head and clutched the steering wheel. I saw Shantel take the money. After I asked her to be the assistant, she said she had to go to the bathroom. She'd been gone a long time, so I thought I should go check on her. Make sure everything was okay. That's when I saw her. She was in the theater's box office, and her hand was in the silver box, rolling up bills and slipping it in her pocket.

I figured Gloria must have asked her to take a deposit to the bank. But, now Gloria accused me of stealing the money. I didn't want my name going down for stealing money, but who was going to believe me when I said I saw Shantel stealing the money?

Slowly, I pulled the truck into the driveway. Blue and green trash cans lined the sidewalks. Trash night is one of my chores. Tonight, I was glad to have something simple to do. I rolled the large green recycling bin down the driveway, and Michael darted out from the back yard.

"You looking for me?" I dropped the recycling bin with a large crash on the curb.

"Nah," Michael said, and kept walking. "You don't seem to need me these days."

I wasn't exactly sure that was true. I'd still like to be friends with Michael. But I wasn't sure how to manage that with his dealing habits. "What are you doing here?"

"Just cutting through," Michael said, "using your yard as a short cut."

Before I could say anything, Michael disappeared. I turned to walk back up the driveway. Alex appeared from the same place where I just saw Michael. Alex clutched his soccer ball in his right hand. His left hand was stuffed inside his short's pocket.

I took four long strides and grabbed Alex by the cuff of his orange soccer team shirt.

"Hey, there," I said. "What are you doing?"

"Nothing." Alex squirmed under my hard grasp.

"How's the eye?" I kept one hand firmly gripped on his t-shirt and peered closer to see that the swelling had gone down. A large purple bruise has taken its place. "You'll live," I said and then, before Alex realized what I was up to, I plunged my right hand into his short's pocket. I yanked up a plastic bag full of small, pink pills.

"Those are mine!" Alex whirled around. He tried to grab the small plastic sack out of my hand, but I was too quick. I inserted the baggie into my pocket. I was a pro when it came to pills and sleight of hand. The pills lay against my leg and all my senses went into overtime mode. I wanted to reach down and touch the pills. Open the bag, take out the magic bullet, and slip it under my tongue. My shoulders tensed. All the emotions of the last few hours would be gone. I could float on an eternal pink cloud.

Alex squirmed under my grasp and jolted me back to my senses.

"He give these to you?" I growled.

"He said they would help my eye," Alex whined. "He told me I could be strong for the next time it happened."

I clenched my fists against Alex's shirt. The rage barreled into me. "Don't go there." I released the grip on Alex's shirt and looked into his eyes. "You understand. Don't go there."

"What do you care?" Alex glared at me. "You're always busy." He looked at my pocket. "I bet you're going to take those."

I stepped away from him. His words hit me in the gut. I did always keep the pills in my pocket. In the past, the pills were a treat I tucked away for those moments when I just didn't feel like I was capable of handling life. I could take one and it would make me feel better than everyone else; like I could deal with whatever life tossed at me.

"Tell me the next time he bothers you." I said gruffly.

Alex gazed at me sadly. I recognized the sadness. Both of us were hurting about Dad. How could Dad be locked up when we were out here? How could we enjoy life when Dad wasn't able to?

"Why don't you help with the show?" I asked. "We could use someone to work with the props."

"You said I was in the way."

"I was wrong."

"Okay," Alex mumbled. "I guess."

The sadness eased out of his eyes, and there was a glimmer of light.

"Rehearsal is at four p.m. tomorrow." I dropped my arm over his shoulder and pulled him to me in a side hug. My breathing was shaky. One more second, and I wouldn't have been there to catch Michael. One more second and Alex might have believed, like I had, that magic lay in a pill.

Alex slipped out from underneath my arm and half-ran and half-skipped into the house.

The pills pressed hard against my leg. I was shaking as I yanked out my cell and hit Marissa's number.

"Got a little opportunity for you," I said as Marissa's sleepy voice answered the phone. "Two tickets to the magic show. Complimentary."

Marissa squealed and told me I was the best. I wasn't the best, I was being manipulative. Marissa would get Michael to the show. And, I was going to give Michael back his little magic sack. I'd tell Michael he couldn't sell to Alex and he could keep his pills. I hung up the phone, and tucked it into my pocket. I fought the craving to use one of the pills. It took all my strength to hold myself back.

CHAPTER TWENTY-ONE

Shantel

Slowly, I got out of the truck. Christopher hadn't said much on the way home. When we got to the farm, he had gotten out of the truck, and opened my door. But instead of kissing me, all he said was, "See you at dress rehearsal tomorrow."

"Sure," I answered, and before I could say anything else, Christopher was pulling out of the driveway, spewing gravel everywhere.

I fought back tears as I walked to the front door. How had this evening gone so wrong? My heart felt like it weighed a thousand pounds as I pushed open the front door. I couldn't wait to get into bed, and lose myself in the world of Regency balls. I'd just reached the staircase, and placed my hand on the wood banister, when Dad called me.

"Shantel. Can I talk to you a minute?"

I stopped and peered back into the shadowy living room. "Why are you sitting in the dark?"

I knew whatever Dad had to say to me wasn't going to be good. The only other time I could remember Dad sitting in the dark, waiting for me, was when I'd been caught shoplifting a silver earring at Summer Market. I hadn't meant to steal it. I was helping Mom sell blueberries and strawberries, and needed a break. I'd slowly wandered down the market stalls, stopping to admire soy candles, homemade baths, and silver jewelry. I clipped on an earring, and that was when I'd heard the commotion. I'd turned around to see a large crowd gathered around Mom's stand, and without even thinking, I'd taken off running. By the time I got there, Mom was swinging her fists at some lady. It'd taken both Allison and Josh, the town's two police officers, to take Mom down to the station, just for a cooling-off period, and drop me off at home. When I got home, Dad was sitting in the dark—waiting for me. He'd gotten two phone calls. One from the police about Mom and one from the jewelry seller about me. He'd spent thirty minutes telling me how stealing wasn't going to help me get into a good college. It didn't matter I hadn't meant to take the earring, or that I planned to return it, the only thing that mattered was I wore the earring.

Now, he was sitting in the dark again. "I stopped by the bank," Dad paused and swallowed. "They told me your college account was empty."

"Empty?" How could my account be empty? I knew the digital reader used up some of the money, and I bought a handful of romance ebooks, okay, maybe more than a handful. And, it was true I'd also ordered a few things online. A few different pairs of shoes and outfits I thought could be useful for other magic shows. Plus some fancy underwear and bras. But did all of that really drain my account?

Dad picked up a piece of paper from the wood table beside him. The bank's name was written across the top.

"I had to buy some books for research," I mumbled. "I guess they cost more than I thought."

"Shantel," Dad said, and shook his head. "I can see what you bought."

I looked away from Dad as heat flooded my face.

"I really wish your Mom was here..." He broke off and stared at the ground.

"Mom," I scoffed. "Like she would help."

Did Dad forget about Mom's "moments"? The time she'd promised to go to my science fair, and then at the last minute, I'd found her lying face down with all the shades drawn. And that happened a lot. Not just for science fairs, but for almost everything. Hair cut appointments, dentist appointments, everything. Mom was never around when I needed her.

Never.

Dad dropped the bank statement to the floor, and stared straight ahead. For as long as I could remember, Dad and I had pretended that nothing was wrong with Mom. We'd gone on like everything was fine. Every time Mom had one of her spells, we all pretended nothing was wrong.

Nothing.

But, the pretending didn't help.

I had to get out of the living room, away from Dad, from his expectations of who I should be and who Mom should have been.

"Why did you need all these clothes? And romance books?" Dad asked softly.

"I'm the Assistant for a Magician," I said.

"Christopher Parks."

"Yes."

Dad nodded. "His Dad was the theater magician. Your Mom and I liked going to his shows."

"You did?"

Slowly, I turned back around. I'd never known Mom and Dad liked magic. They'd never talked about it. In fact, I couldn't remember that Dad and Mom ever went out. Especially as Mom got worse.

"Yes," Dad said. "I suppose it's not quite how I imagined you. But," he stared at the ground, "nothing is turning out how we imagined, is it?"

"No," I said. "It's not."

The next day at dress rehearsal, I wondered how the show would ever pull together. Gloria was running around with a clipboard and a pencil tucked behind her ear. She kept calling out, "Don't worry. Dress rehearsal is always chaotic. It means the show is going to be fabulous." I didn't believe her. A tap dancing group ended in tears when one of the girls tripped and sprained her ankle. A boy who was supposed to be performing a serious monologue erupted into serious giggles. And a small dog that was a part of a hula hoop performance got loose. Practice came to a grinding halt as the theater erupted in chaotic shouts, giggles, and laughter as everyone chased the dog.

Before the rehearsal, Gloria pulled me aside and said the police were going to stop by and question Christopher. "No one is arresting him," she said. "They just want to question him."

I wanted to tell her the truth. The words were on the tip of my tongue. But I couldn't make them form. What would happen if I told? What would happen to the show? No. It was best to wait until after the show. I just hoped I could get to Gloria before the police got to Christopher.

I gritted my teeth and repositioned myself inside the small basket. Above me, Alex handed Christopher a small sword. "Not that one." Christopher grumbled at Alex for the hundredth time.

I couldn't believe Alex was going to be a part of the show. Did Christopher want us to fail? We'd practiced and Alex still couldn't seem to find the right magic prop at the right time. I'd thought it was just a case of pre-show jitters. But when Alex continued to bring out the wrong magic toys, even though Christopher laid them all out on the table behind stage while explaining the correct order, I began to think Alex had some other problem. It was taking all I had to grit my teeth and not blurt out that Alex should only watch the show.

"We should just skip this one." Christopher muttered. His eyes were wide, and I saw the worry in them.

"No," I insisted. "It'll work out. We need to practice." We hadn't practiced the girl in the basket. Christopher said that we probably wouldn't need the trick. But I wasn't so sure. What if the audience loved us? What if we had to do an encore? Christopher had shown me a video tape of his father performing the basket trick. I was supposed to squeeze myself inside the small basket. Then, Christopher would insert swords through the narrow slits on each side. "Real swords," he'd said. This wasn't like the "girl gets sawed in two" trick where the swords were fake. This was the real thing. The trick was only to be performed by master magicians who could handle the real swords. As Gloria said, this wasn't a birthday party trick.

"Go on," I said and crouched down on my knees. "Get the swords."

Reluctantly, Christopher pulled the top over me. "Everything okay in there?"

"Yes," I called as the darkness engulfed me and, for a minute, a heavy sense of panic settled on my chest. What if I missed guiding the swords into the small slits? What if one slipped and cut me? No, I told myself. Don't even think about it. Everything is going to be fine. "Everything's great," I yelled.

Carefully, I moved my hand along the inside of the basket. I located the first slit to the right of me. I moved away from the opening as much as I could and held my hand up in a cupped position. The sword would glide past my hand and towards the opposite side of the basket. It seemed very simple—as long as I didn't remember the swords were real.

"And now I will insert this sword," Christopher said outside the basket.

The sword whizzed close to my left ear and toward the other side of the basket. I reached out to grab the long handle and guided the sword into the small opening opposite me. It wasn't so bad. Okay, I was shaking a bit. But, really, it wasn't so bad. I tucked my legs under me and ignored the aching cramp in my left thigh. It would all be over in less than a minute.

"The second sword," Christopher continued.

I hunched over and reached out as the second sword zoomed into the basket. The space had gotten significantly smaller. Now, I understood why Christopher was reluctant to try this trick. He'd said that as a child, he had been his Father's assistant and the trick was designed for someone who was tiny enough to maneuver inside the small space of the basket when all swords were inserted.

I wiped my sweaty hands on the top of my shorts. I tried not to think about the swords. Instead, I focused on Christopher.

Over the last week, Christopher had conquered the straightjacket trick. It had taken him hours and hours of practice, but he was able to do it. Then, we both mastered the woman who gets sawed in two. Now, all we had to do was practice this trick a few times, and we'd be the stars of the evening.

"Not that one!" Christopher snapped.

"I can't find the other one," Alex whined.

I held my wrist up and quickly checked the time on my watch bracelet. Each act had fifteen minutes for practice. Gloria wanted dress rehearsal to run as close as possible to the real show. The point, she said, is to not only to make sure you can do your act, but that you can work with the other acts in getting on and off the stage. I heard Gloria's voice above the din of commotion in the theater, "That's enough. Rehearsal's over. Everyone scram. Show opens at seven p.m. tomorrow night. All acts must be here no later than six-thirty."

Christopher's face appeared at the top of the basket. "Climb out," he said. "We're not doing this one."

CHAPTER TWENTY-TWO

Christopher

It was show time, and I paced outside the theater door. My top hat wobbled while my cape flew out behind me. I looked like a madman, but I didn't care. My heart raced a million beats per second, and I craved the small pills in the sack tucked inside my pocket more than I thought was possible.

I checked my watch one more time. Where is Shantel? It was way past six-thirty. Crowds of people streamed in the front doors. Even Mom had already arrived.

"Hey, Mom," I said as she accepted a program from Alex, who stood at the theater's double doors. Alex wore dark slacks that were too short, and a white short-sleeve dress shirt. His shirt was too tight and it stretched across his thin chest. It was pretty obvious Alex hadn't worn dress-up clothes since last Christmas. Mom placed her hand over her bright red lips.

"It's okay." I stepped forward to stop Mom from grabbing Alex and hauling him to the car.

"It's not okay," Mom practically shrieked. "Look at him. He looks like no one cares about him."

"It's not that bad," I said. "He's going to be helping me with the props. No one will see him."

"But he's out here," Mom exclaimed. "I just can't believe this. Why didn't you tell me?"

"It's okay, Mom," I said. "Really. It'll all be okay." Mom was bothered about more than Alex's clothes. All of us are. Dad's ghost is in every corner. I'd gotten stares and a couple of well-meaning hugs with soft words of, "I'm so sorry." Mostly

I was ignored by people who I thought were Dad's friends. For Mom, this wasn't any easier than it was for Alex and me.

Mom slumped before she reached over and adjusted Alex's shirt. She leaned down to kiss him, and said, "I'm proud of you." Then, straightening she looked at me. There was a tear in the corner of her eye. "I'm proud of you, too." Before I could say a word, she joined the crowd moving inside.

I swallowed the lump in my throat. Mom was proud of me. I'd done something right. I was sober, and I was performing magic. The world was brighter and I grinned at Alex. "We're going to be great," I clapped him on the shoulder.

At the same time, there was a hand on my shoulder.

"Good luck, Christopher. Break a leg."

I turned to see Charlie and what looked like the whole home group meeting. Everyone in a large cluster behind me. I swallowed and thanked everyone for coming. As the group entered the theater, I tapped my left foot on the sidewalk in a little jig. Where is Shantel? I looked down the street toward the empty and silent bakery. I thought Shantel was getting ready with Mia. But there wasn't any sign of life in the bakery. I checked my watch again. It was almost seven p.m.

Gloria stuck her head out the theater door. Her hair draped over her shoulders and she wore a long skirt and flowered blouse. Her eyes were bright and her cheeks flushed. Gloria was in her element. "Where's the Assistant?"

"I don't know." Bile rushed up in my throat. I couldn't go up on stage without Shantel. There was no act without Shantel.

"Your act is last," Gloria said as if she could read my mind. "Don't worry. There's time." She frowned at two men wearing khaki pants, with button down dress shirts, and small phones clipped to the outside of their pants. Immediately, I identified the men as undercover cops. I could pick them out anywhere. They wore plain clothes, but they might as well be wearing cop outfits. It was something in the walk. Their eyes shifted everywhere.

I stuck my hand inside my black dress slacks and felt the plastic pill baggy as it slipped through my fingers. My plan was to give the pills back to Michael whenever he showed up with Marissa. Then, with one swift phone call, I would tip off the police to his whereabouts, sit back and watch as he got hauled off to juvenile detention for possession. But now, I realized that I wouldn't be able to follow through with the plan. The cops would watch me, see the exchange, and haul me off to detention.

Michael's low-riding silver Honda, with the shiny wheels, cruised slowly down the street. His car jerked to a stop in front of the theater. Marissa exited and slammed the passenger side door. She draped something that looked like a coat which should be in the theater's costume box, around her shoulders.

"Marissa," I said. "Isn't it a little hot to be wearing that?"

"He's such a jerk."

"What now?" I muttered.

Michael's car screeched away and turned toward the freeway.

"He's not coming." Marissa spit the words out of the side of her mouth. She linked her arm through mine and sidled up to me. Her thin body pressed against me, and for a minute, the overwhelming flowery smell of her perfume choked me. "But, I'm here," she purred.

CHAPTER TWENTY-THREE

Shantel

Mia tossed another black sandal out of her closet. The shoe added to the growing pile on the hardwood, bedroom floor.

I slipped a black flat on my left foot. "Do you have a match?"

In the living room, Jeffery read to two-year-old Owen. His deep voice boomed while Owen's small one giggled in response. I wondered what they were reading. Mom always read to me. She changed her voice to match each character. It was like seeing a stage performance every night.

Performance.

Quickly, I checked my watch. It was almost seven.

"Mia, we need to go."

"Here it is!" Mia held up the matching, simple low heeled black sandal.

I grabbed the sandal out of her hands and slid it on my right foot. I should have known my beautiful, shiny, high-heeled sandals were too good to be true. I'd barely stepped out of the bakery and was trying to walk down the sidewalk when my heel got caught in a grate. It was lucky I managed to untangle myself without breaking an ankle. My shoe hadn't been so lucky. It lay, with the heel snapped, in the sidewalk grate.

Drew walked out of the coffee house, and ran over to help me. "What are you doing?" Drew grabbed hold of my arm. "Why are you dressed like this?"

Drew's eyes dropped to my lacey top which, showed more cleavage than I remembered when I tried it on. I tried to adjust my shirt higher, and explained I was going to be an assistant for the magic show. Drew's ears and face turned red. "Magic?"

"You should come," I said. "It's at the theater. Tonight. At seven pm."

Drew glanced down the street. His face looked like he'd never seen the theater before. "Okay." His face turned an even darker shade of purple. He thought I was inviting him on a date! I was too upset over my ruined high heel shoe, to try and explain to Drew. He'd come to the show. He'd see Christopher and me. He'd know. I hoped he would know. And if not…if not, I could figure it all out after the show.

Once I hobbled back to the bakery, Mia took one look at me, closed the shop, and drove me to her apartment where she'd been hunting for matching sets of shoes for the last fifteen minutes.

"Mia." I tapped my foot. "I'm late."

"Right!" Mia hurried to her feet, grabbed her purse, and dragged me into the living room. As soon as Owen saw Mia, he started whining. Mia looked at Jeffery who hushed Owen by picking him up and rocking him back and forth.

"I've just got to run her over to the show. I'll be right back," Mia said.

"You're not coming?" I asked.

"Sorry, hon," Mia said to me. "Jeff has to work tonight. I've got to get back."

"But you knew…" I stopped. I was whining. Mia had responsibilities, other things besides me and the magic show.

Mia hustled me into the car. She slipped the keys into the ignition. The car turned over, and Mia pulled out of the apartment parking lot. "How are you doing with everything?"

"Fine." Okay, so maybe breaking my high heel in the sidewalk grate wasn't the best way to start the evening, and I was a little late, but I was feeling okay. I had a small case of pre-performance jitters, but I didn't feel sick.

"Really?" Mia looked over at me and then back at the road. "Because I thought you might be a little upset."

"About a shoe?"

"It's just anniversaries can be hard," Mia said. Her fingers clutched the steering wheel.

"Mia," I growled, and clenched my teeth together.

Mia pulled hard on the wheel and stopped on the side of the road.

"What are you doing?" I shrieked. "I'm late."

"You're the last act," Mia said calmly. "I'm more worried about you."

"Drive!" I reached over and yanked on the steering wheel.

Mia pushed my hands away and turned to face me. I stared straight out the window.

"Shantel," Mia said. "You've got to face it. There are going to be anniversaries, birthdays, and you can't keep pretending."

I looked out the window into the darkness. I knew what Mia was trying to tell me. But, I didn't want to think about it. Not now. I turned away from her and crossed my arms over my chest. "Could you please take me to the theater?" I said quietly.

Mia shook her head, and started the car again. We drove the rest of the way to the theater in silence. The car rolled up to the curb and I saw Christopher. Christopher and Marissa. How could I miss them? They were so close together. Were they kissing? I didn't want to look.

Mia stopped the car. "Are you okay?"

"I'm fine." I stepped out of the car and walked past Marissa and Christopher. Neither one of them saw me. But, I heard Christopher say, "I'm not kidding, Marissa. He was selling to Alex. I've got the pills and I'm giving them back to him."

Before I could think about it, Gloria stuck her head out the theater doors. "Last call." The lights flickered inside. A gust of wind barreled around the theater's side wall, and my hair fell out of the barrette. It had taken forever for me to fix my hair and it was all unraveling with one gust of wind.

Without saying anything to Marissa or Christopher, I headed toward the front door.

"Shantel!"

Christopher stepped up beside me and I shivered.

"Here." Christopher shrugged out of his black magic cape and, with a large flourish, draped it around my shoulders.

I took hold of the cape and our fingers met. I looked up into his bright blue eyes. "Thank you," I said. In that moment, I vowed that as soon as the show was over, I was going to confess I stole the money. It was me. Not Christopher. I was going to begin to tell the truth and that would start with confessing about stealing the money.

Christopher held the door for me, and gently pushed Marissa toward the balcony. I couldn't help but smile. Marissa couldn't sit with us. The performers had a reserved section in the front.

By the time we got to the seats, there were only two spaces left. I squeezed into the middle of the row and sat down. Christopher did the same in the row in front of me. I settled into the red plush seat. It was hard not to pay attention to Christopher. His hair curled over the top of his white dress shirt, and he smelled like a deep spicy woods.

The show started. Gloria was right. The disastrous dress rehearsal was in the past. Each act went off without a hitch. There were no tears from the tap dancing group. The dog stayed well-kenneled until her part of the show, and the moving on and off of each act went smoothly.

And, then, all too suddenly, it was our turn. I was standing onstage, just like we practiced. And when the lights went up, I couldn't see anyone past the first two rows. From behind the curtain, Alex handed us the various parts just as planned.

Smiling, and playing my role, I helped Christopher into the straight-jacket and stepped aside. I carefully made sure my face showed just the right amount of surprise and not too much too early or too late. The audience loved us and each act received more and more applause. Before I knew it, we were at the end of the show and I was lying down for the woman who gets sawed in two. As practiced, I tucked my feet up and under me as the box split. The sword seemed to go right through me. I smiled as thunderous applause erupted in the theater. Christopher repositioned the box and I unfolded myself. I slipped my hand into Christopher's and took my position next to him. I knew we had done it. Our act was the final highlight—just as Gloria wanted it to be.

"You're a hit!" Gloria stepped out of the wings and grabbed both of us. She pushed us forward and with a loud stage whisper said, "Encore."

"A what?" I called, and then feeling swept up in the emotion of the moment, turned to Christopher and said, "We have to do an encore."

"No." Christopher shook his head.

"Yes," I said, and without even thinking, I called for Alex to bring the basket and swords. We could do it. I could feel it. It was like the game of pretend. The moment was here. And all we had to do was pretend we knew what we were doing. Everything would flow together. "Just pretend," I leaned over and whispered to Christopher. "It'll all be fine!"

"We didn't…" Christopher tried to shout over the applause. But, the noise was deafening and his words were lost.

I pulled open the basket top, and smiled at Christopher. I ran my hand down his cheek in a gentle caress. In a bold move, I leaned over and kissed him. Hard. On the lips. The audience went wild and, I climbed inside the basket.

Everything would be okay, I told myself. Christopher was my boyfriend. I trusted him. I crunched inside the wicker basket and curled my legs underneath me. I wiped my sweating palms onto my black slacks. The audience stopped calling for an encore. They were so silent I wasn't sure anyone was still out there.

I'd barely gotten my balance before the first sword barreled into the basket with a lot more force than we'd practiced. Startled, I realized Christopher was keyed up from the magic show performance. He was overestimating the force he was putting behind the swords.

I tried to figure out how to tell him to slow down. I couldn't very well call out to him or the audience would hear.

Before I could it figure out, the second sword zoomed past me and into the basket. The two swords crossed over my head, and I rearranged myself so I could crouch lower. As I shifted, a third sword whizzed by my left arm and peeled off a small layer of my skin. I saw the blood before I felt the searing pain.

"Christopher?" I said weakly. Everything around me seemed to be very warm and very blurry.

"The final sword." Christopher said from outside the basket.

This time, the sword dropped onto my left leg and sliced off another long stretch of skin. I fell against the side of the basket and it tipped over. The lid rolled off and I sprawled out onto the stage floor. Christopher lunged toward me. He yanked a handkerchief from his pocket, and a small plastic baggie, filled with pink pills, dropped onto the stage.

"Arrest him!" Dad shouted from the back of the theater.

The world went dark.

CHAPTER TWENTY-FOUR

Christopher

I slipped my foot into a thick orange sock and plastic sandal. I took a scratchy blue juvenile detention center blanket from the pile in front of me.

"One."

I walked down the fluorescent lit hallway behind the guard. The walls were the same concrete we have at school. Did someone get a deal on vanilla concrete? Everything went down quickly after Shantel got hurt. All the cops needed was the drug baggie which dropped out in plain view. Nobody even mentioned the stolen money. I couldn't look at Charlie or the guys from AA in the front row. I didn't want to think about Mom, or all the people who held their programs and whispered.

"Shame. He's just like his Dad."

"One to One East"

The guard looked into the cameras on the ceiling above us. As if by magic, a heavy door opened. I walked inside and the door clicked behind me.

"Ten A," the unit guard barked. The unit was a wide open room with small cell doors lining the side walls. In the far right hand corner of the unit, one of the doors clicked open. I entered the cell and choked on the sharp smell of ammonia that permeated the space. I tossed my blanket on the bed. The concrete walls were painted beige. The bed was a thin mattress tossed on top of a wood slab. I didn't have a roommate. I have to work up to level five before I get to share a cell. I turned and gagged when I saw the steel toilet next to the bed.

"Parks," the Unit Officer barked. "You will join us."

I exited my small cell and walked into the large unit. Ten boys sat around hundred pound tables. The tables were heavy so no one could toss one in a fit of rage. But, the chairs are light, and I could easily hurl it across the room. I pulled out a chair and to my surprise Michael said, "We all end up in the same place, bro."

"Thought you were out on business."

"Got caught." Michael shrugged. "Picked up for speeding. Found a few things in the car. Heard there was a good show at the theater. Sorry I missed it."

"I was waiting for you." I spit out the side of my mouth so the guards won't see us talking.

"Here I am. You found me."

"You were selling to Alex."

"Your brother is no different than you. He wants it just as bad."

I shoved myself away from the table. The chair scraped the floor and the guard barked, "Parks! Quiet!"

I clenched and unclenched my fists. I tried to control my rage and stared at the tabletop. There was a checker board painted on the top. I doubted they would let us have the small checker pieces to play. I seethed. Alex did not want the drugs as bad as me. And if I had anything to do with it, he would never, ever find out how those drugs made you feel. The highs or the lows.

The unit doors clicked, and I expected to see another detainee, but instead, a woman entered. She carried a canvas bag, and the guard directed us to clear the space for poetry workshop. Obviously, the woman had been here before because instead of the room erupting into jeers and groans about poetry, everyone made a space for her at the table.

"You got the new book?"

"Is my poem going to be in the new book?"

I was never a fan of poetry at school, but, the energy in the room was contagious, and I leaned forward on my arms.

The woman took out a stack of books and placed them in the middle of the table. "Everyone can take one," she said.

"To keep?"

Hands grabbed frantically. Even Michael, and he was never into poetry at school. I waited until the frenzy died down before I reached over and took a book

"I see some new faces," the woman said. "My name is Madeline. I'm a writer and once a week, I write poetry with you. It's poetry from our experiences." Her voice sounded like it had a smile tucked inside.

Madeline made eye contact with me, and I quickly looked away. I'm not sure why. It wasn't like I did anything wrong. But, there was something about her that made me feel transparent. It was an uncomfortable feeling.

Madeline handed out lined paper and small stubby pencils and asked if anyone wanted to read poems from the book. I expected to hear silence. But instead, a couple people volunteered to read. I shook my head and flipped open to the first page. This must not be like ordinary poetry.

A boy started reading, and right away, I felt like crying, and at the same time, I wanted to hide away under the table. I never heard anyone lay it on the line the way these poets did. It was like being in an AA Meeting, except this time everyone was a teen, and telling it like it really was. There was no hiding in this poetry, no talking about marriages or kids. Instead, these poets talked about girlfriends they let down, mothers and sisters they disappointed...and, what hit me the hardest, fathers that aren't around.

And, I wasn't the only one, because everyone at the table went really silent. Even Michael was staring at the tabletop and not saying much.

"Why don't we write about fathers today?" Madeline suggested. "If you need prompts, how about 'I always wanted to tell you....'"

I expected someone to say something. At school, when a teacher gave an assignment, there was always at least ten minutes of conversation about the assignment. But here, nobody said a word. They just took the paper and pencils and started writing.

I stared at my blank paper.

There was a lot I wanted to tell Dad, but mainly I wanted to tell him I was sorry. Sorry I went to rehab. Sorry he had to steal to get me to rehab. Sorry he got arrested.

"Can we start with I'm sorry?" I asked.

"Sure." Madeline smiled at me. "The idea is just to write what is on your mind."

"Do we have to read these?"

"No," she answered. "We'll have time for sharing. But nobody has to read them if they don't want to."

"Okay." I felt safer. If we didn't have to read the poems aloud, I could tuck the writing into the manila school folder, and forget about it.

I started jotting down lines.

The hour passed quickly, and pretty soon Madeline asked for people to share. At first there was silence, but then, a boy who had been pretty quiet volunteered to go first. He read a poem about himself as a father. I took another look at him. He didn't look older than twelve, but I know looks can be deceiving. Right away, another boy volunteered to read and Madeline suggested we go around the circle. We could say pass if we didn't feel like sharing.

One by one, everyone read their poems. Even Michael read a poem. Michael wrote about how his dad is always working, and how Michael thinks he's probably having an affair. I was surprised. I've known Michael a long time, but we never talked about stuff like that. When Michael was done, he slid the poem towards Madeline. "Maybe you'll pick it for the next book?"

The circle reached me, and all eyes were on me. My palms were sweaty, but I knew I had to read. It was just like the Meetings. Everyone shared their poems. Everyone had the courage to read what was in their heart. It was my turn now. I picked up my paper, and it shook. I cleared my throat, but even then, it felt like I had sandpaper inside of me. I started to read. The words felt sticky in my mouth. But, as I read, I gained strength and by the end of the poem, my voice sounded normal.

"It's not your fault," Michael said when I finished.

"What?" No one else had commented on anyone's poem, and suddenly I felt really vulnerable.

"You got a disease. You're an addict," Michael said clearly. "Your Dad stealing that money didn't have anything to do with you. That's his problem. Your problem is you have to stay clean."

I locked eyes with Michael and it was as if we were young again. No anger. No drugs. Just him, telling me the truth. It was like they said in Meetings. The people around you could see the truth of your disease better than you.

"Thanks," I said, and gave him a nod.

"Time's up," the guard said.

There was a flurry while Madeline gathered papers, pencils, and encouraged everyone to keep the poetry books.

We stood and pushed back our chairs. Michael was still watching me. And, I heard his words in my head. "Not your fault."

When we got into our small cells after dinner, I was still thinking about the poetry workshop. I read a couple more poems from the book Madeline gave us, and then I stared at the ceiling. I was an addict. I admitted that I was an addict. I need to stay clean and sober. Dad is not my responsibility. Dad stole that money because Dad has a disease too. The disease of the "high." The high came from lots of places. It could come from a drug, but it could also come from getting away with something wrong or illegal. Something like stealing.

The last magic trick played in my mind, flashed before me in full color.

The wild look in Shantel's eyes when she insisted we do the basket trick. The way she kissed me and ran her hands down my cheek. In front of everyone in the theater. Shantel stealing money, and then, how I didn't tell anyone. My stomach hurt with the truth. I was enabling Shantel just like Jarrod enabled me on the baseball team. Shantel behaved like an addict. But, like Dad, she's not my responsibility either.

My responsibility was to stay sober. It wasn't my fault other people had problems. That was something I heard at Meetings, and it never made sense until now. I didn't cause Dad to steal. I couldn't control his sickness by trying to be the perfect son, or by trying to convince other people to think I wasn't not like him. No one could help me, until I wanted help. It was the same for Dad.

And I couldn't help Shantel.

Shantel had to face the truth herself.

Something inside me lifted. Something I had been holding onto for a very long time. And even though I was locked inside the small cell, I felt freer than I had in a long time.

CHAPTER TWENTY-FIVE

Shantel

I held my bandaged arm to my side and loosely clutched the small piece of paper which had my prescription for pain medication. While Dad signed the hospital release forms, I struggled against my memories of Mom. The smell of antiseptic. The sound of patients being rolled down the hall. The nurse's soft whispers. Ever since I was admitted to the hospital, it'd been like being sucked into a vortex that drew me down, deeper and deeper. My limbs felt heavy. It had nothing to do with the pain medicine.

"Where is Christopher?" I asked weakly. It'd been so chaotic at the theater. Gloria wrapped the fluffy dresses around my arm and leg, and Dad yelled. I vaguely remembered the baggie with the pink pills lying near my head, and a scuffle between Christopher and some men who I didn't recognize.

"The police arrested him." The nurse handed me a small, plastic sack. My lace top was stained with dark blood. I'd never wear the shirt again. "Drugs at a family show." The nurse shook her head, and tucked her lips into a tight line. "It's a shame he's so much like his father."

Dad placed his hand on my lower back. "I'll get the car."

"Wait," I said weakly. Christopher hadn't been planning to use the drugs after the show. I'd heard him. He told Marissa the drugs belonged to Michael. He caught Michael trying to sell them to Alex.

"Dad," I said. "Christopher didn't—"

"Not now." Dad shook his head as he guided me to a bench

and pushed me, not so gently, down into the bench. "Wait here."

I leaned my back against the concrete wall. The sounds of the lobby swirled around me, and a memory. A memory I couldn't block. Dad and I...side-by-side. We leaned against each other, in the orange plastic chairs. Waiting for the nurses, the doctors, for anyone to tell us what was going on.

I was the one who'd found her. She was lying upstairs on her bed, her arm draped onto the floor, and an empty bottle of pills beside her. "Mom?" I asked. I knew immediately something was wrong. Mom's black moods took her into long and deep sleeps, but she'd never looked like that. So still, so emotionless.

I'd done everything to try and forget that memory, and yet, here I was. In the same hospital, the same lobby, the same bench. I sat here when the doctor came out. I'd known there wasn't any hope. Mom had taken her black and dark mood, and spun it into a spiral so deep and dense, it would impact Dad and me forever.

There was no insurance money. There was no life insurance. There couldn't be. Insurance policies did not cover suicide. And we lost the farm.

"No," I cried out and held onto the bench. I didn't want to remember losing Mom to her illness. But, I had created my own illness. I refused to see what was true. Instead, I created elaborate fantasies. Fantasies which, I thought, kept me safe from the possibility of real life.

But those fantasies made me hurt someone I loved—Christopher. I was the one who insisted we do the trick. I was the one who created an elaborate romantic fantasy about Christopher. He wasn't a hero in a romance novel. He was a boy who was trying to stay sober, and I was not helping him. I was lost in my own whirling addiction of fantasy.

As Dad's car pulled up to the curb, I knew what I had to do. I had to tell the truth to everyone. I had to tell about the conversation with Marissa and Christopher. I had to tell the drugs didn't belong to Christopher. And, I had to tell I'd stolen the money from the theater.

I swallowed hard. But even more importantly, I had to let Christopher go. It was time I faced life on life's terms—without my romantic fantasies. It was time to let go of pretending and be honest.

ONE MONTH AFTER

Shantel

The late summer sun cast shadows across the sidewalk. I dunked my paint brush into the glass jar of water, and added the last bit of green to the heavy wood board. I leaned back to admire my work. It wasn't going to win any awards, but the farm scene had come out pretty well.

"Can you help with this?" Gloria gasped. She lugged the woman-who-gets-sawed-in-two prop onto the stage.

I rose to my feet and stared at the box as if I was seeing a ghost. The summer was almost over and already the days were getting longer. In another week, I'd be back at school again. I wasn't sure what everyone was going to think about my new schedule. I'd been sentenced to a hundred hours of community service for stealing the money from the theater's box office. Everyone thought it was a fair sentence. The hours meant I'd had to rearrange my schedule. I couldn't take my traditional eight hours with a six a.m. early class. I would be spending my early morning hours volunteering at the child care center where Mia's son, Owen attended.

Slowly, I walked toward Gloria and released the wheels on the box.

"Easier," I said. "It rolls."

"The Assistant knows all the secrets." Gloria pushed the hair out of her eyes. She smiled at me. "Why don't you roll it to the door? Someone is coming to get it."

I rolled the box down the ramp of the stage and up the aisle. I made my way carefully so the box didn't bump into anything. It wasn't heavy, just awkward to maneuver.

When I reached the theater door, I stopped.

Christopher stood on the walkway. One half of a stepping stone rested in his palm.

I clicked the lock on the wheels and stepped into the garden pathway. I found the other half of the stone where I'd placed it. I looked Christopher in the eye and said softly, "I believe these belong together."

Christopher chuckled. He stepped toward me and gently pushed the hair away from my face. He ran his finger lightly along the side of my face. "I believe they do."

And then, the vision cleared, because this wasn't a romance novel, this was my life, and life wasn't a romance novel. No matter how much I wanted to pretend.

A heavy set man strode toward me. "That the magic box?" he asked.

"Yes." I released the wheel and rolled it toward him.

The man grabbed it with a small grunt. "I got a good deal for this box. Going to take it to Portland and use it in some shows."

The man wheeled the box down the ramp and, looking across the street, I saw the tall, blond boy come out of the church. A group of men gathered around him, and I could hear the laughter as it drifted across the street. He didn't look at the theater, and I didn't call out his name. Instead, I turned around, and walked down the garden path beside the theater. A green glass tile poked out from under a pile of dirt in the flower bed. Carefully, I leaned down, wiped away the dirt, and placed the two mosaic stepping stones side-by-side.

"Shantel."

Turning slowly, I watched the tall, blond boy jog across the street, and I smiled.

Because this time, this time, he knew my name.

And so did I.

ACKNOWLEDGEMENTS

The following people supported and encouraged me while working on this story: Vermont College MFA advisor Liza Ketchum said, "I think Shantel and Christopher both have a story." My fabulous critique partners: Rhay Christou, Jennifer Spray Doering, Ann Teplick, Sundee Frazier, Holly Huckabee, Prosper Barter, and Gayle Bellows. The YA Book Group: Pamela Greenwood, Nancy Vittor, Carole Daag, and Kristen Hendricks-Fonseca. WendiLee MacLeod and Susan Goettsch at the Volunteers of America Children of Promise Program, and my mentee, Faith Dye.

Robin, Chris and Thom who were once teens in recovery; the teens at Denney Juvenile Justice Center who tell their stories so honestly in the poetry workshop; Gary Marks, Henri Wilson, and Margie Holloway for support; and Jim Willie who taught me about high school baseball.

This story never would have been possible without the Fellowships of AA and Al-Anon. The Seattle RWA Chapter opened my eyes to the world of writing romance, and especially e-publishing. Thank you to Director Tamara Thompson and Danielle Gomez at Serious Take Productions Marketing for your fabulous cover. And finally, thank you to Kelly Shorten at KMD Web Designs for the book layout and formatting.

EXCERPT FROM STAINED GLASS SUMMER...

Chapter One

"Art Power," Dad says.

I move my finger over the amethyst oval stone set inside a silver ring that looks very expensive. I've gotten used to Dad's outrageous, impractical art presents, like the tall, pink glass vase he gave me last Christmas. It's part of being an artist's daughter, and I love it.

"Fabulous!" I've been waiting to use that word on something after I heard an art judge at one of Dad's shows exclaim, "Fabulous!" when she handed him the first place ribbon. I wave my hand over Dad's photography books on the coffee table and admire the carved leaves and swirls that don't completely cover my tanned ring finger.

"It's too expensive for a twelve-year-old," Mom says as she enters the room. She carries a white cake with twelve candles. Her dark hair bounces with every step. It's the same color as mine, only hers is curly and mine is straight. My eyes meet Mom's, and I look away. I know she's right. Dad's gifts are too expensive. But I love Dad's fabulous art gifts, and I'm not going to give them up.

"Wish for a win in that contest," Dad says as Mom sets the cake on the coffee table. His eyes sparkle as he leans forward. I notice the small bit of gray in his hair that frames his narrow face.

I know not to say anything. Dad doesn't believe in getting old. I think about the school art contest. The winner gets to take summer classes at the Chicago Art Institute, where Dad teaches. I'm already imagining what will happen when I win. I'll spend the whole summer with Dad. We'll ride together to the Institute, and I'll take my classes while he teaches his. Afterward, we'll ride home together and talk about our day. But even more importantly, I must win to prove that I'm an award-winning artist like Dad.

My stomach cramps as I think about trying to prove that I am an award-winning artist. I take a deep breath, and lean over to blow the candles. All of the candles blow out, but one remains. Its flickering flame is like a taunting tease.

"Oh no," I moan. "It's bad luck!"

Dad exhales, and in one whoosh he blows the last candle out. He turns to me, and his eyes are cold and unreadable. "I trust you to take good care of the ring. The Andes artist says it has power."

"Seeing the future?" I run my hand over the purple stone. The stone warms under my touch, as if powers are seeping from the ring's stone into my hand and back again. I'd love to see the future. I rub my finger over the smooth stone and wait for Dad to tell me about the ring. I love Dad's travel stories. He entertains Mom and me with world adventures in different languages, new customs, and exotic foods.

"Power," Dad says. "Power for your art."

"Mmm…" I say, hoping I sound very serious. I know about art power. There can be nothing on the canvas, yet there are a million things waiting to be born. Art transfers me out of one time and into another. I love to look at the clock and, when I check again, five hours have passed. Some days the ideas come rushing forward while other days nothing comes at all. But I always like the surprise of never knowing when the ideas might pop up.Mom clears her throat, and I look up to see her holding a piece of cake on a sunflower paper plate and a Happy Birthday napkin. As I take the plate, our fingers touch, and I grin. Mom stopped at the bakery down the street to pick out the most expensive cake in the store. Mom likes expensive presents just as much as Dad does.

I lift my fork to take a bite and watch as Mom tries to hand Dad a piece of cake. He frowns and shakes his head at her. For a minute, a hurt look darkens Mom's face. It's the same one I feel when he has something else to do and I'm annoying him. Something that happens a lot and I try not to think about.

Dad doesn't notice Mom's look. He never does. In Dad's world, there is one person— Dad. Mom and I say that is what makes him such a good photographer. But sometimes I wish that he weren't such a good photographer, and a better dad instead.

Dad stretches. His six-foot frame reaches toward the high ceilings, and I swear that if he stands on tiptoes, he can reach the ceiling beams with his long, tapered fingers. "I'm headed upstairs."

"Can I come with you?" I ask softly, and stare at the floor. I can't look at Dad. There's too much hope inside me. Hope that too often goes unfulfilled.

"Just for a little bit. I want you to finish up that collage for the contest. I'll make sure everything looks perfect."

"Everything looks great!" I pop off the couch and leave my untouched piece of cake on the coffee table next to Dad's photography books.

"Jasmine." Mom touches my arm briefly, and I want to shake her away. I know what she's trying to tell me. Don't get too excited. You know how he is. This moment isn't really about you; it never is. It's about Dad. But I don't want to hear her, not now. Not on my birthday. Instead, I want to believe that this moment is about me. I want to believe that this time will be different.

"The contest," I say, while hoping Mom understands my unspoken words. It's okay this time. "Dad has to help me finish my collage."

Mom shakes her head and turns away from me. She reaches to the coffee table beside her. "I have something for you too." Mom turns around, holding a thick catalogue between her fingers. "I wanted to surprise you." She pauses and then says, "I bought you special summer school lessons."

"Art classes?" Mom bought me art classes! I am so excited I can barely breathe. My birthday is turning out to be fabulous.

"Not exactly." Mom shakes her head, and her dark brown hair moves from side to side across her shoulders. "These classes are at the private high school. It's the school where I attended." There is a bit of hesitancy in her voice, as if she's worried I won't remember all the times she has told me about her high school. "I thought you'd like to get a head start for when you're ready for high school. If you start now in summer classes with a foreign language, then in a few years you'll be very prepared for the high school classes."

"Oh," I say, trying not to hurt Mom, but it doesn't take much to hear the deflation in my voice, as if I am a balloon that has just lost all its air. I twist my fingers together. I do appreciate her gift. But I am an artist. I need summer art classes with Dad, not classes at Fishers.

"Fishers is a good school," Mom says quietly.

"Please, Mom," I beg. The words tumble out before I can stop them. It's a conversation Mom and I have had a zillion times. No one ever wins.

Mom slowly sets down the catalogue. She lifts her plate and takes a bite of her cake. Her red painted lips close over her fork as the cake slides into her mouth. I've disappointed her, and I feel bad. Most of the time, Mom and I are a team. We have to be. It takes two of us to live with Dad, and even then, I'm not sure we ever really win.

I try to explain to Mom. "You'll see. I'm going to win the contest. It will all be okay." I reach out and give Mom a small pat, as if she is the child and I'm the adult. "I promise. It will all work out."

Mom smiles sadly at me. "Okay, Jasmine," she says.

I twirl around and head toward the loft spiral stairs. I know that, this time, things will work out.

As I climb the spiral staircase into the studio loft, I hear Dad walking above me. I can't help but hum. I love nighttime in Dad's studio. It's taken me a long time to earn Dad's trust. On my first visit to the studio, I tried to color on one of Dad's paintings. I thought the white box outline in the middle of the white canvas needed some color. Dad caught me as I was busy scribbling away. He grabbed my hand, and the crayon dropped to the floor. He didn't say anything for what seemed like forever. And then, with his voice of steel, said, "If you're going to do art, I will teach you."

Now, I watch as Dad pours hot water from a small silver pot that rests on a warming plate in the far right corner of the loft. "Hot chocolate?"

"Yes." I head for the rack of mugs perched on a shelf below a window overlooking Lake Michigan. There are mugs with scenes of Australian beaches and oceans, and other mugs with African lions, giraffes, and elephants. I pick up one of these mugs and hope the power of the animal will jump off the cup and I'll roar.

I pour hot water from the pot and eye the row of Dad's pictures hanging on the white wall. A small light highlights each. I know each photo by heart. Each framed picture has a blue or silver award tacked to the frame: Best New Photographer for the State of Illinois, First Place in the Mid-West Photography Winter Exhibit, First Place in the Chicago Photography and Design Show. The rows stretch twelve across. This spring, Dad has started hanging a second row under the first.

"Yours will be right next to mine," Dad says when he sees me looking at the pictures. He points to a blank space. There is a hook already attached to the wall.

I bite the inside of my cheek and taste a small amount of blood. I have to win the contest. If I want to be an artist like Dad, I have to start my own wall of awards. And, even more importantly, I have to prove that he has the best daughter in the world, and the only way to do that is by winning art contests.

I turn around and look at my contest entry, which is laid out on a long easel. Dad has been helping me and adding touches while I haven't been in the studio, but something doesn't seem right. He's added a bit of texture for a three-dimensional appearance. But I'm not quite sure that the colors blend in the far right hand corner. I want to say something to Dad, but I know what he'll say. "In order to compete, you must stand out. Yours must be different than everyone else's."

I rub my fingers over my new ring's purple stone and hear a whisper. I'm not sure if it's my imagination, but I think I hear the stone say, "You will win the contest." Dad said it had magic powers.

"Are you going to get started?" Dad asks. He perches on a metal stool with a brown cushion in front of his computer. He waves his hand toward the canvas.

"Just thinking." I smile at Dad. "Preparing." Dad always says that half of art is preparing — thinking about what you want to accomplish before you sit down and start to draw.

"Well, don't prepare all night." Dad checks his watch. "I need to sleep."

I'm suddenly nervous again. I know the rules. In the art studio, we follow Dad's rules.

I dip a large paintbrush into green paint and wipe the edges against a water jar. For a minute, doubts crowd my mind as I study my painting. Dad chose an extra-large canvas from the art shop. I'm not sure how I'll get the canvas to school without a ride, and getting a dependable ride from Dad is not always easy.

"I just got busy," he'll say as I open the car door, after forty minutes of waiting outside the Art Palace Community Hall on Saturday mornings. It's always embarrassing, waiting for Dad. The last Art Palace teacher to leave always asks if I'm sure that I didn't need a ride home. And they always give me that look. It's the one that is half-pity and half-worry, while I try to make up excuses for where Dad is and why he forgets his daughter.

I once tried to be mad at Dad about his lateness, but as soon as I got in the car, he turned to me and said, "Don't give me attitude or I won't pick you up at all." The last thing I want is for Dad not to pick me up at all.

I love my time with Dad — even if he is a little late. I study my painting and say softly, "Dad?" "Mmm…"

"You're taking me to the school contest tomorrow, right?" Dad stops and raises his eyebrows.

I know this look and it frightens me.

"Why are you asking?" Dad snaps. "I told you I'd take you. Don't ask again."

"Right," I say as my stomach churns. I don't know why I asked. I knew Dad would take me. Sometimes I just do stupid things. This time, I have broken Art Studio Rule Number 2: No disturbing the artist at work.

I shift on my stool and turn my attention back to the painting. There is something about the colors that doesn't sit right with me. In my mind, I picture them alive and vibrant. But on the page they seem dull and flat. I stare out the window and into the tall dark trees surrounding the studio. If only I could capture the green, or even the amber, orange and yellow when the oak tree leaves turn in the fall.

And then, as if a genie has hopped off the tree and said, "Your wish is my command," light green, dark green and leafy textures swirl around me. It is as if I have left my body and I am flying in the trees. It reminds me of when Dad takes me to the amusement park and I ride the roller coasters. When my heart beats a million miles an hour, as the small carts careen close to the edges and around loops but always, held by a small chain, holding me above the hard ground.

In my art trance, I am flying up and down the tree limbs. I reach toward the sky and then, sensing that I can't crash into the ground, dive back toward the roots of the tree. Everything buzzes, hums, and vibrates around me in a symphony of sound as I dance on one limb and then the other. I am flying in tune to my own harmonized orchestra.

The studio casts light into the tree and I fly over to the window. Dad shifts and moves images on his computer. My mind whirls. Am I really in the tree? How has it happened? I feel so free. It's as if possibilities are all around me and nothing can stop me. Every artist must know this feeling! The green fades, and my hands grasp my paintbrush. The paint smell of the studio engulfs me.

"Dad!"

"Yes?" Dad doesn't take his eyes off the computer screen.

I stop. What will Dad think when I tell him about this world?

But I can't keep it in. I have to tell him.

"Yes?" Dad repeats and peers at me over his thin-wire rimmed glasses.

"I danced in the tree limbs. Everything was so green! Can you do that?" I hop off my stool.

"Maybe it's the muse," Dad says. "Or maybe it's part of that magic ring. You know I always choose great gifts for you."

"Yes," I say. "You always choose great gifts." I twirl my ring as I think about where I have just been. The world is my own private art world. I can go there anytime I need ideas or inspiration. It's a bit like magic, and now I must give the world a name. When I was younger, I lined up all the stuffed animals on my bed and gave them each a name. Not just a first name, but a last name too. I chose names that sounded exotic to me, names like Hamish and Rhianna.

The name for my magical art world has to be something special. Something unique. Something like…Lucianna. The name pops into my head and I remember Lucy Ann, my best friend in elementary school, who arrived in second grade with a new pink pencil case, sharpened colored pencils and fresh watercolor paints. She was my best friend until she moved at the end of fourth grade, and I haven't had another friend like her.

"Jasmine," Dad says, his voice suddenly sharp. "Get back to work. I've got some other things to do."

I nod as the familiar feeling of not wanting to bother Dad washes over me. I don't want to annoy Dad. I'm not always important to him, but I want to be.

I drop a splotch of green onto my canvas. The paint spreads

out, leaving thin spider legs behind like cracks in a sheet of glass. I can't help but think that I am like a sheet of glass, cracking under the pressure of Dad.

To read more of Stained Glass Summer you can find a copy at most book retailer.